THE BLACK HORSE TAVERN

THE BLACK HORSE TAVERN

*New revised edition
with an Introduction by the author*

Raymond Fraser

Lion's Head Press

The Black Horse Tavern was originally published in 1973 by Ingluvin Publications. All the stories from that edition have since been revised by the author. Individual stories were published at various times in The Journal of Canadian Fiction, Tamarack Review, The Fiddlehead, Ingluvin Magazine, Intercourse, The New Brunswick Reader, and Ellipse (with a Spanish Translation). The present revised version of "The Quebec Prison" was included in the author's book *The Grumpy Man*.

Library and Archives Canada Cataloguing in Publication

Fraser, Raymond, 1941-, author
The black horse tavern / Raymond Fraser. -- New revised edition. / with an introduction by the author.

ISBN 978-1-928020-00-4 (pbk.)

I. Title.

PS8561.R3B5 2014   C813'.54   C2013-908249-2

Lion's Head Press
Toronto • Canada

CONTENTS

INTRODUCTION

In another book of mine, *When The Earth Was Flat*, there's a memoir dealing with the years 1970-1972 in which among other things I talk about the publication of my first book of fiction, *The Black Horse Tavern*. At the time I was living in Montreal and doing story readings in high schools and universities with a group of five writers (Clark Blaise, Hugh Hood, John Metcalf, Ray Smith and myself) under the name The Montreal Story Tellers. Here's how the part about *The Black Horse Tavern* went:

> "Hugh Hood was having his latest book published by Oberon, and he informed me that Michael Macklem, the publisher, was interested in my work... he'd personally liked the manuscript of a novel I'd sent him the year before, even though he'd rejected it on the advice of others. He told Hugh he'd like to see a collection of my stories. I wrote Macklem and got back a nice encouraging letter. Encouragement was just what I needed. So what if I didn't have enough good stories for a book? I soon would have, just watch.
>
> I sat down and in a couple of months wrote "The Quebec Prison,"

"They Come Here to Die," "On the Bus," "A Cold Frosty Morning," and "The Janitor's Wife"; and adding some earlier things and titling the lot *The Black Horse Tavern* I put the manuscript in the mail.

And in a while it came back. Rejected again... If I was in a bad state before, and I mean by my reckoning, my crazy inner world, it was mild to how I felt now—because while I was never sure about the other works, I *knew* this was a good book. It was the best I was capable of right then. I hadn't been lazy or self-indulgent, I'd taken my time and revised carefully and objectively. This time I was right for sure, and *they* were wrong. So after all it wasn't me—it really *was* them. That was more than disheartening, it was scary. If I was right and everyone else was wrong, that meant in effect that I was wrong—my entire perception was out of whack, my standards meaningless. To double-check I sent the manuscript to Doubleday, and got another rejection. The hell with it.

I wasn't going to throw in the towel, I was too stubborn; but what could I do? A violent frenzy seethed inside me. I couldn't stand it. Naturally

I had to drink—if I didn't thoroughly anaesthetize myself I might do something catastrophic. Every day I sat at the kitchen table guzzling beer and going over in my head how I could rob a bank. If I had money... with money I could start a publishing house, put my own books out. I didn't know how to get money any other way. I cased the banks, outlined getaway routes, dreamt up disguises—I worked it out in detail, all the fine points, the plan getting thorough and elaborate. But what if I got caught? I doubted I could handle a long stretch in prison. For one thing they didn't let you drink there, and I couldn't possibly survive without drinking. It would be better if I were killed in the attempt.

I couldn't be sure I was only fantasizing because I could feel myself getting nuttier every day, more cornered and desperate. Something had to happen one way or another.

For reasons unfathomable by me, God who knows every hair on our heads has been in the habit of intervening in my extremes to keep me writing, and out of jail, the madhouse and the grave. I had made my yearly application to the Canada Council, but my hopes were of the slimmest kind, considering the way I saw my luck as running. But I was hanging in to find out, it was the last card being dealt in that particular hand. I hate to think what the next deal would have been had I not got the grant; but as it happened I did. There was no elation this time, only a grim consciousness that I'd had a narrow escape, miraculously saved at the last instant. A very sober reaction—rare for me. Being crazy, however, a mocking voice in my head kept saying, "Your cup runneth over, your cup runneth over." It wouldn't stop, going on maddeningly. "But it doesn't," I answered. "Stop saying that." I knew what I had now was an opportunity, not a reward. I couldn't act frivolously with this money; in my condition I was convinced my life depended on putting every penny to work.

My first act was to call Kenneth Hertz and ask his advice on getting a book printed. I was aware that doing my own book would involve numerous problems, and lies, and probably humiliation—"So nobody else would touch it, eh? Had to put it out yourself. Ha Ha!" Like some old spinster and her religious verses blowing her savings at a vanity press.

I should say that after Doubleday I hadn't sent *The Black Horse Tavern* to another publisher because I felt it would be a waste of stamps. I was full-up with rejections, no room for any more. I had almost forgotten I'd given Hertz a copy of the manuscript one day when he dropped by. He had a small publishing outfit called Ingluvin, and some time after he told me he would like to do the book, but he didn't know when, he had other commitments, maybe someday... that sort of thing. It could take years if ever, and I had no patience; I'd never had any, but now especially I felt I couldn't wait much longer. Better to see to the job myself, then I could be sure it would get done.

When I called him he said, "I don't know why you want to publish it yourself. I said I'd do it."

"Yeah, but when?"

"Well, I'm almost finished with Pat Lowther's book. I can get to yours next."

He sounded as if he meant it. I wanted to believe him, because the way I am, once I consider doing something almost any alternative looks better. I project catastrophic outcomes. Here was an appealing option, the job taken out of my hands. I'd get my book done and have my money too. What more could I ask for?

"They're good stories," I said. "You won't be embarrassed."

"I know. I like them."

"You mean you read them?"

"Of course I read them!" He sounded quite indignant. "Do you think I'd publish something I hadn't read?"

"I suppose not."

It must sound strange, but I'd come to believe that what you wrote had nothing to do with a publisher's decision. I didn't know how you could influence those people, if they were people. Maybe they flipped coins or cut cards or threw darts at names on the wall. If it was the case—as some maintained—that you had to know one personally, then perhaps it followed that the content and quality of your work wasn't a factor.

Now that I could see some light I thought possibly I'd come around a hairpin bend and was on the way out of the noxious tunnel I'd been stumbling around in. But it was an elusive light, a false light actually; things didn't really get any better for the next ten years. The story of when and how Ingluvin eventually published *The Black Horse Tavern* would discourage I don't know how many would-be writers. But it did finally come out in the spring of 1973, and I'm grateful to Kenneth Hertz for it."

Once out the book was actually quite a success, by Canadian standards. It received excellent reviews in newspapers all across the country. John Richmond in the Montreal Star wrote: "Rattling good yarns without managed thrills and contrived tension, *The Black Horse Tavern* is the reflection of a man who has lived a life far from quiet desperation. Like Fraser's poetry, it is relentless, subtle, disturbing, bearing the stamp of immediately recognizable talent and nifty writing." In the Montreal Gazette Betty Shapiro wrote: "All ten stories in *The Black Horse Tavern* bear the Fraser touch: gutsy realism, originality, and humour. The effect is hilarious, moving, and sad. It's quite a book." And from Alan Dawe in the Vancouver Sun: "A highly original voice that is occasionally sad, sometimes very comic. A real pleasure to read."

Farley Mowat read it and called me "the best literary voice to come belling out of the Maritimes in decades." Alden Nowlan wrote that Raymond Fraser is "one of the most gifted writers I know, and among his gifts are two that are all too rare: a zest for life and a sense of humour." And the novelist Hugh Garner predicted I'd "make it big" one day.

The point of this being, the book was exceptionally well received, and not just by critics and a number of prestigious writers (of whom I've named just a few), but by the public, those who got to read it. And yet despite that and the fact the edition of 1,600 copies sold out fairly soon, it was never reissued. Ingluvin Publishing folded not that long after, and no other publisher ever expressed any interest in doing it.

Until now, as you can see, some forty years later.

A few words about this new edition. In order to get it ready for publication I had to scan (in the technological sense of the word) the text, since it dated from the days when writers used typewriters and not computers, and while checking the scan over for mis-reads (of which there were many) I inevitably chanced on words and lines and passages that I felt could be improved. Some of the stories didn't need much: I barely touched "College Town Restaurant", "The Newbridge Sighting", "Bertha and Bill, and "Spanish Jack". "The Actor", on the other hand, a very early story dating back to when I was a student at St. Thomas University, I altered to the point of leaving it out altogether. While it possibly showed some promise for a young writer, to bring it up to where it would satisfy me today I felt would take too much effort. By way of compensation I replaced it with a slightly modified version of a longer and later story called "Man With A Flair". This story is in another book of mine, *Rum River*, but as it's set in the Black Horse tavern it seemed a logical choice for inclusion.

Other than "The Quebec Prison", which is a novella and much the longest piece in the book, the story I altered most was "The Janitor's Wife". In it's original form it contained two stories running parallel, one in regular text and one in italics. I took the italicized part out, not just because the story is better without it – a fairly good reason in itself – but because I later used an improved version of it in my novel *The Madness of Youth*. When the italicized part went however, so did the "the janitor's wife" – she was no longer a character in the story, so I had to give it the new title of "Lennie's Girl". "Lennie" because I also changed the protagonist's name from Frankie to Lennie, which I thought suited him better.

All of the stories in the book take place in the nineteen-sixties and seventies, but that's no knock against them. Outside of science-fiction all novels and stories are either set in the past or, like people, end up there eventually anyway.

R.F.

They Come Here To Die

1

Since the Black Horse was the only tavern in town it was not a good thing to get barred from it if you were a man who liked to drink and socialize. For about the hundredth time Ralph Ramsey was barred. "This is it, Ralph, out you go! And this time it's final, don't come back again." MacPherson the waiter escorted him out the door and slammed it behind him and Ralph staggered away in the night. For some reason his pal Sully wasn't with him. It wasn't often they weren't together.

"What'd he do this time, Mac?" I asked the waiter a few days later.

"Oh, he got up on the table ranting at everybody—'You're all full of shit!' he says. 'You're nobodies! You're nothings! What has any of you ever done, eh? Tell me that? What kind of mark are you guys gonna leave behind when you're dead? You're all full of shit!" You know what he gets like, the man crazy, he should be put away."

Other times Ralph had been barred for bumming money around the tables, or playing his trumpet, or breaking glasses, or starting fights, or any combination of these things. His friend Sully had been barred with him a few times, but Sully was not so unpredictable, he was less given to explosive outbursts. By himself it's unlikely he'd have been barred more than a few times.

A couple of weeks later, in the normal course of events, the two of them would drift in the door and sit quietly in the corner. "Okay if we have a drink, MacPherson? We just dropped in for a quick one."

MacPherson was by nature a kind and easy-going man, and by this time would have forgiven or forgotten about the last incident, and he'd serve them like any other customers in good standing.

Although it may sound like Ralph was a wildman, he wasn't. He was only that way sometimes, when he had too much to drink, and even then only when the mood struck him. Otherwise, drunk or sober, he was a sensitive and thoughtful person. It would be hard to say his age, he was one of those individuals who seemed to have always been around Newbridge, a fixture like the Black Horse itself, or the town hall, or the Catholic church. He may have been forty, perhaps not much more than thirty-five. Then again he might have been forty-five. He had a moustache and a closely-cropped beard and thick hair that poured down over his collar. This was in the early sixties and Ralph's appearance was then considered rather eccentric, as was his general behaviour.

18

One day, in fact it was the afternoon of Christmas day, he dropped in to my place while I was doing the dishes. It was a freezing wintry day but he had no coat on. He looked haggard. "I didn't sleep a wink last night," he said, taking a seat at the kitchen table. "I can't sleep anymore. I never could. I don't know what's wrong with me. I walk around all night and then when daylight comes I go home and go to bed. When everyone else is getting up I'm turning in. Every night it's the same. The cops are starting to look at me. One of these days they're going to arrest me."

"Arrest you? What for?"

"I don't know, for something. For impersonating a human being." He had a laugh at that.

It being Christmas there was a bottle of rye sitting on the table. Ralph eyed it a few minutes, then said, "You don't mind if I have a taste of that."

"Here." I poured him a drink.

"That's nice stuff. Very smooth. Did you get that for Christmas?"

"Yeah. From myself."

"I got some liquor too. I mean my mother did. No, I guess it was me. I was at home last night and there were gifts under the tree, and I thought, this must be mine, *Evening in Paris*, so I drank it. Yeah, I got lots of booze. It's all gone now, I drank it last night. The old lady doesn't know yet. *Chanel No. 5*, that's another one. One of these days I'll go into some posh bar, I'll be standing there looking sophisticated, and the bartender'll say, 'What's yours, sir? What are you going to have?' 'Oh, I guess I'll have an *Evening in*

Paris. On the rocks.' It's so long since I had the real stuff I forget what it's called. Shaving lotion, vanilla extract, rubbing alcohol—perfume! As long as it comes in a bottle that's the important thing. You can't drink the labels."

He'd brought his trumpet with him, which was about the only thing he owned, apart from his clothes. "I want to play you a number," he said, "something in season." He put the trumpet to his lips and played *O Holy Night*—In a small room like my kitchen it almost blew the roof off. He was a good musician at times, when it suited him. He'd been playing the trumpet for years and years, ever since he was a boy. Several times he attempted to play with local dance bands but it never worked out. He couldn't read music and he had his own ideas about arrangements, and he had difficulty keeping sober. He claimed the other musicians were unimaginative and mediocre, which they probably were. He was, you might say, an artist who relied on inspiration, and his temperament made it difficult to adjust to other musicians and regular dates. So now he played for himself and his friends and once a year entered the Sanitorium Fund amateur night where he was always a big hit but never won a prize.

"Thank you, Ralph, that was very nice," I said.

"I lost my teeth last night," he said. "I had all my teeth pulled a few months ago and got a plate, but I left my coat somewhere and my teeth were in the pocket. Dr. Reid pulled all my teeth out—Look." He opened his mouth, revealing the bare gums. "He said he was going to give me a plate—I told him, why not throw in a cup and saucer while you're at it, a plate's no good by itself. This is great stuff. You don't mind if I have another one?" I poured him another rye. I remember Ralph saying once he'd gone to a doctor because he thought he had ulcers, and the doctor wanted to know about his drinking habits. "He gave me this test, it was a list of twenty questions to find out if someone's an alcoholic, and if you answered yes to four of them that meant you were. There were things like, Do you drink because you feel shy with people, Do you crave a drink in the morning, Do you drink to escape worries or troubles—there were twenty of them, and I answered yes to them all—except one. And that was, Does your drinking interfere with your work? I put down no for that one." Ralph hadn't had a job since he was a teenager and worked part-time at the ginger ale works sorting bottles.

He took a pull on his glass of rye, then sat there a moment silently. When he spoke his voice sounded suddenly sad. "No work, no money, no women, nothing," He said. "I've got the feeling I'm just watching life go by and I can't do a thing about it." He shook his head. "I came here to play a song and have a few drinks and be happy, but it's no good. You know, everybody around this town thinks I'm a bum. Everybody does. I can't get a girl, not a chance. You want to know something that happened? I asked a girl out a couple of weeks ago. I said, how'd you like to go out with me some night, we could go to a show or something. Do you know what she answered? I wouldn't go to the shithouse with you. How would you like it if a girl said that to you? That's pretty bad, eh? A girl has no right to say that to a man, no matter who she is or what she thinks of you. But that's my status around here. Just because I don't have a job and live like everyone else... I'm an individual—I don't have to do what everyone wants me to do. I may not have much in this life but I've got my own mind. What I should do is get out of this town. I should, but I don't. Why don't I just get out? Tell me that?"

"I don't know. It's up to you."

"I guess so." He was quiet again. Then he said, "Well, I'll have to go home and see my mother and father. Then it's back to my own estate on Water Street. My parents, they watch me like two cats to see I don't step out of line. But I'm always drunk just the same. I've got nothing else to do. I'm an alcoholic. I can prove it, just ask me twenty questions. I drink and I don't do anything else."

"How much do you drink anyway, Ralph?"

"How much? As much as I can get. I'd be drinking twenty-four hours a day if I could afford it. But I've got no money. I'm living on welfare. Did you know that? Me, on welfare. What do you think of that? I get sixty dollars a month. I give my mother and father forty and keep the rest. So I have to go bumming on the streets to get enough for a drink. That's how low I've come. I bum money down on the front street. A bum." He got to his feet, still holding his glass with an inch of rye in it. "I have to try and find my coat. My scarf is in the pocket, and my teeth. But I don't care about the teeth. I hardly ever wear them anyway."

"They must make eating easier."

"No, I don't eat with them. They aren't comfortable. They're just decorations. I only wear them at special times, like when someone asks me out." He laughed. "Yeah, when I'm asked out, that's the only time I wear them. Anyway, I've got to get going. What time is it now? I'm going blind, I can't even see that clock there."

"It's twenty-to-five."

"There, I'm late already." He emptied his glass and at the door shouted over his shoulder, "Merry Christmas and a Happy New Year!"

There was one detail about Ralph's visit that I didn't pay attention to. Shortly before leaving he went to the bathroom. When he came out he didn't stay around much longer. I learned why the following afternoon.

Ralph was at the door and came sheepishly in. "The thief returns to the scene of the crime," he said.

"Yeah?" I didn't know what he meant.

"Ah me. I'm cold sober. I woke up this morning ready to put down a big drink of rum, I had it hid away under the bed, and I was thinking by God it's good to have a drink in the morning, I need one real bad, and I've got a pint of rum sitting there under the bed. A pint of rum!" And he started laughing to himself. "Yes, that's the way to start the day. I had it all figured out. I didn't touch the pint last night, saving it for the morning so I could start the day off right. Well, that's what you get. Crime doesn't pay! The thief returns to the scene of the crime."

"What are you talking about, Ralph?"

"Have you got a beer? You wouldn't have a beer in the house?"

It being the season the fridge was stocked, so I got out a couple of pints of Schooner.

"Ah, that feels good, nice and cold. Yes sir, I unscrewed the cap and was set to bolt down a big drink the first thing in the morning. By God it's a good thing I didn't. Turpentine! That's the way to start the day—with a good shot of turpentine. Here I thought I had a nice pint of rum and it was turpentine."

Now I understood. My bathroom was quite a mess, and among other things lying around was a bottle of turpentine which I used for cleaning paint brushes. If you didn't know what it was you'd think it was booze, because I had the stuff in a rum bottle. Ralph had spotted it when he went to take a leak and thought it was the real thing.

"You mean—you stole that bottle of—"

"That's right. Ah, what a person I am, I've got no scruples, I come here and drink your liquor and then try to steal more of it. I must have no shame, no conscience at all. I hated to do it. But I saw that pint there and I thought this is just what I need for the morning. Perfume in the evening and the real stuff in the morning. I got up and reached for the bottle this morning with my hands trembling and I took the cap off and started to take a drink. That's what I get. Turpentine! It's punishment for my sins."

Well, we had a bit of a laugh at that and drank a lot of beer. At some stage in the afternoon Ralph once again bemoaned the fact that he was reduced to nothing but a bum and an alcoholic. "I went to the AA's for a while," he said, "I tried to kick the habit. But that's no good. They can't help me. I remember one meeting, you know the way these things go, this guy got up on the platform telling us his life story, what hell his life was when he was drinking and why he had to stop. I don't even know his name, he was some guy from upriver, I never saw him before. This was the first night that Jackie Craig—he'd never been to a meeting before and somebody had talked him into going and he was standing at the back of the room—you could tell he wasn't happy about being there by the look on his face—and this guy up front was saying when he drank he used to beat up his wife and children, really kick them around, little kids and all—he was giving a big description of the terrible things he used to do, and he was going on and on about it, when there was this disgusted voice from the back of the room: 'You rotten bastard. You're not an alcoholic—you're nuts!' It was Jackie. Soon as he said that he turned and walked out."

It was fall, late October, this particular time Ralph got barred from the Black Horse. Being barred wasn't all that much an inconvenience, there were plenty of places to drink provided you could come up with the price of a bottle. Ralph's old room, for example, in the old Kelly rooming house by the Ferry Wharf—a place he despised—or on one of the wharves, or in a boxcar at the CN station, or behind the stores on Water Street where the ground was covered with broken wine and rum bottles. But in the cold weather it was better to be indoors, and in the King George there was always someone there and Ralph enjoyed company.

Much of the time his company was Sully Sullivan. Sully was around my age and so a lot younger than Ralph. He'd left school at the age of sixteen and since then had done as little in the way of work as possible. A day in his life can be described simply enough.

He lived with his parents, and around noon he would get out of bed and have a couple of strips of raw bacon and a bottle of coke for breakfast, then head off for the pool room. He'd spend the afternoon shooting pool or playing the pinball machines or if he was broke he'd watch others do these two things. If someone came up with a bottle of something he probably wouldn't go home for supper. If not he would go home and eat, saying not a word to his mother and father. They had stopped saying words to him as well, after years of talking at deaf ears. The only exception was once every two or three months when there would be a row over his not getting a job. This accomplished nothing and another several months of silence followed. His father had got him work once as a house painter but Sully lasted only to his first pay cheque, which he blew in two nights of drunken generosity towards his friends. This brought him to the realization that working didn't pay—not two weeks of backbreaking labor for a two night drunk—so he failed to return to the job on Monday, or ever after.

After supper it was down town again where he quite often bumped into Ralph on the street. If there was any money they pooled it and caught the liquor store before it closed. If there was none or not enough they spent the next few hours bumming, or they hunted around to find someone who would buy a bottle for the pleasure of their company, usually some teenager just starting to drink. Then they made for one of the many bootleggers in town.

When the night ended Sully went home to bed. Every day it was more or less the same story.

Sully was Ralph's close associate for several reasons. One, he had the same amount of time on his hands; two, he had an attraction to the bottle; three, he was a misfit and knew it, just like Ralph; four, he wasn't, despite his limited education, all that stupid and Ralph could talk to him; five, they shared a fervent dislike for the town and almost everyone in it.

2

The night after Ralph was barred from the Black Horse for his tirade from the tavern table he was down in his room by the ferry wharf. It was a miserable rainy October night, the kind of cold rain that hits your skin like frozen needles. Ralph's room was on the second floor at the back corner of the building. It had two windows, one facing the river and the other looking down on the lane leading from Water street to the ferry slip. There was a streetlight at the lane corner and at intervals sheets of water gusted past the light. Except for the weather outside this could be any night of the year. Ralph was standing looking out the window, hands behind his back. Behind him lying on the sunken bed with both shoes planted firmly on the blankets was Sully. "Well, what are we gonna do?" said Sully, for about the half-dozenth time.

"I don't know, we can't go out in this. Why don't you go up to the tavern."

"Fuck that. If they won't let you in, the hell with them. They're not gonna get my business. Besides all I got is a quarter. We could go up to the Castle." The Castle is a restaurant in Bannonbridge, a teenage hangout where they do much of their panhandling.

"Won't be anyone there tonight. You'd have to be crazy to be out on a night like this. It wouldn't be worth the walk."

When they were silent you could hear the rain, and from a room above a record was playing *I Walked in the Garden with Jesus*. When it reached the end whoever was playing it started it over again. The same hymn has been repeating itself now for over half an hour.

"You know, that could drive you batty," said Sully, staring up at the ceiling. "Who lives up there anyway?"

"I don't know, I don't know anybody in this place. They're all old people," said Ralph. "I'm the only one here under seventy. I don't know where they all come from. I see them creeping up and down the stairs and along the halls. They just look at you but they never say anything."

Sully fished a package of tobacco from his back pocket. He rolled a cigaret and the shredded end flamed briefly when he lit it. "Be great to have a drink now," he said.

"I'm glad you came over," said Ralph, still staring out the window. He shook his head. "What a goddamn dismal depressing sight. I can't stand being alone in this room anymore, I'd rather be in jail. At least you'd know why you're there. I'm serving a sentence and I haven't been arrested yet. Solitary confinement. It's nice to get a visitor."

"I don't blame you. I couldn't take this place very long myself," said Sully. Ralph's room, it was true, didn't have much to recommend it. It was like a large box papered with brownish wallpaper with yellow stains seeping down from the ceiling. The ceiling itself was a network of cracks and places where the plaster had fallen revealing wooden slats. The furniture was a bed, a wooden chair, a small chest of drawers and a table which was now covered with dirty dishes and utensils. The lightbulb was weak giving the place a dusky atmosphere. There was no heat and both of them kept their coats on.

Well, what'll we do?" said Ralph.

"Play something why don't you. Anything to drown out that noise upstairs."

Ralph took his trumpet out of its dog-eared leather case. Different times he'd been on the verge of selling it, feeling there was no important reason for keeping it, he wasn't going anywhere, but each time he hadn't been able to go through with it. He knew that once gone it was unlikely he'd ever get the money together to buy it back or get another one.

"What do you want?"

"Play Ruby."

Ralph blew on the trumpet but his heart wasn't in it. He stopped after a short while. "I don't feel like it. I'll play it later."

"That was good, that sounded real good. I wish to hell I could play a trumpet like that, or anything, even a mouth organ."

"Well, you're not too bad a singer. That's enough."

"Yeah, I can sing, I'm not a bad singer. Maybe we should form a group, just the two of us. We might go places."

Ralph paced the short distance across the room and back. "It's going to be another cold winter. You know they don't have any heat in this building? If you want heat you have to buy your own heater. Last winter—it was like a refrigerator in here last winter. I can't afford a heater. There should be a law against this, it's no way for a man to live. It might be all right for an Eskimo. But I'm not an Eskimo."

"You can already see your breath."

"And look at these, storm windows they call them, they're supposed to keep out the cold. French safes, they nail big French safes across the windows and leave them on all year and you're protected from the cold." There were plastic coverings over the windows, they had stretched and sagged and they flapped in the wind and distorted the view outside. "You can't take your clothes off in the winter, I went months and I couldn't take my clothes off for fear of dying of exposure. I wasn't warm one minute for more than six months. That's a hell of a way to live. I don't want another winter in this hole. I'd rather live in an igloo. What I should do is make myself an igloo this winter and live in that. Even an Eskimo wouldn't live under these conditions."

"At least it's a place to have a drink, it's a good thing they don't bother you that way."

"They don't care what you do. All they care about is your rent."

They heard the sound of slow feet shuffling in the hall, passing the door and ascending the stairs. They listened until the footsteps are gone.

"Another old man," muttered Ralph. "This house is full of old men, they all come here to die. I shouldn't be here. I'm not an old man. I don't belong here."

He picked up his trumpet and blew a deafening defiant blast. A sharp knock sounded on the wall.

"Who's that?" said Sully.

"Another old man. Or maybe it's an old woman. They don't like to hear me playing at night—or anytime for that matter. They want to die quietly."

"What we need—we ought to get out of here, that's what," said Sully. "I mean out of town. We're wasting our talents here, especially you, not so much me since I don't have too many, but I'm getting sick of this place. I'll never get anywhere in a dump like this. We should just get up and get the hell out, just like that. No wasting time."

"Where would we go?"

"Anywhere. Montreal. No, Toronto's better, Montreal's full of crazy Frenchman, we'd never get anywhere there. Toronto."

"You can't go anywhere without money, Sully. How would we get there? What would we live on?"

"It wouldn't take much. I could probably steal enough off the old man to get us started. We take a train up and then we find a job. We could live good up there. The wine's cheaper and there's lots of loose women hanging around. It'd be no problem."

"I don't know anything about Toronto, Sully. They'd never give me a job, a guy my age."

"You play the trumpet, eh? There are hundreds of bands in Toronto, they're always looking for talent. Look, Ralph, for Christsake, you can't wait forever. I mean, around here they don't know a trumpet from a shoe horn—you're crazy hanging around Bannon-bridge."

"I know, I know." Ralph pondered a moment. "You're right, I have to get out of here, that's the only solution. I can't just sit around this town and die." A moment later he said, "Ah, it's no use. We'd never make it . You need money, you need connections, we'd be lost in Toronto."

"C'mon, don't talk like that. I thought you wanted to leave."

"Sure. Sure I want to leave."

Sully got up off the bed and with a long snorting snuffle inhaled his nose clean and spit into the grocery bag Ralph was using for garbage. "Well, make up your mind. I'm ready to go."

"I don't think you are, Sully. If I said, okay, let's pack, you'd make up some excuse for putting it off."

"No, I wouldn't." He settled himself back on the bed.

"You know, the worst thing is that they don't give you a chance," said Ralph. The wind and rain were shaking the plastic storm windows, snapping them against the inside windows. "They're only interested in themselves. Well, I don't give a shit about them. Who are they anyway? They're a bunch of nobodies."

"The hell with everybody," says Sully.

"All they want to do is push you into the dirt, they aren't satisfied unless you're crawling in front of them."

"It's no good talking about it. My Christ, I wish we had something to drink, I'm croaking. I should've asked the old man for a few bucks." He adjusts the pillow under his head. "But I wouldn't give the bastard the satisfaction."

"It's not that I'm not good enough. It's not that."

"You're *too* good for them. They can't stand that."

"I just don't get a chance. I'm getting old, I'm an old man now."

"C'mon, Ralph, you're not old. You're a young man. You got a lot of time left and you got the talent. What've I got?"

"Pass me your tobacco."

Ralph rolled a cigarette and lit a match with his thumbnail. He dragged on the cigarette and fingered his beard. "I think I'll shave this off," he said.

"What?"

"The beard. I'm going to shave it tomorrow."

"How come? It looks good. Don't be crazy."

"I don't care. I need a change. Maybe I'll try and get a job. That'd be a change, I mean if I can get a job."

"Maybe I should get one too."

"But who'll hire us? They think we're bums."

"The hell with them."

"No, it's no good. Maybe if I shave nobody will know me. They might hire me that way. I could say I'm a stranger in town. What do you think?"

"The hell with them. The best thing to do is to get up to Toronto. There's no future hanging around here. I could be your manager."

"Yeah, my manager. That's what I need, a manager. Okay, you're hired."

"How much of a cut do I get?"

"I'll give you fifty per cent. How's that sound? Fifty per cent of nothing."

"No, I'm serious."

"Okay, I'll pay you in advance. How about..." He reached in his pocket and pulled out a ball of paper which he opened. It was a two dollar bill. "How about fifty per cent of a bottle of wine?"

"Hey! Where'd you get that? Here we've been sitting around here—"

"I got it from my father to buy a pair of gloves for the winter. I was up to see him this afternoon. But I don't need gloves, it's not my hands that need to get warm. I can always keep my hands in my pockets. I'd only lose a pair of gloves anyway."

"How come you didn't tell me? I mean we been sitting here dying of thirst—"

"I don't know. I guess I promised him I wouldn't drink the money..."

"Give it to me. I'll go up to Old Sal's and get a bottle."

"No, I'll go with you, I don't want to stay here, I'm sick of this room. I'd rather be out in the rain."

Ralph pulled the string on the light and opened the door. The hall was musty smelling and the only light was from the ground floor below. They went by a shadow standing at the head of the stairs, they could hear the laboured breathing, one of the old men who lived in the house.

"This place gives me the creeps," Sully muttered going down the stairs.

Water was streaming over the street and the rain hit them like icicles. All the way up Water Street there wasn't a soul in sight, it was like a ghost town. The wind whipped the rain at them.

"Where we going to go once we get it?" said Sully. "We can't stay out in this." They walked along quickly with hands in pockets and shoulders hunched into the rain.

"We can sit in a boxcar."

"It's kind of cold."

"A few drinks and we'll be all right."

"Yeah."

THE QUEBEC PRISON

Flight From Montreal

Have you heard this one? About the major league ball player who thought he could sing? He put a record out and it was a dismal failure. Naturally he was quite annoyed and he began complaining to his agent, and his agent, a philosophical man, said: "Oh well, you can always go for a walk."

"A walk?"

"Sure. A walk's as good as a hit."

Yes, I know, that's not much of a joke, even if you're familiar with baseball expressions. All the same I get a slight charge out of it. The reason is, I made it up by myself. Like an after-dinner speaker I wanted to start off with a joke, something to catch your interest and put you in a pleasant, hence vulnerable mood.

My name, by the way, is Alex Buckley.

I invented one other joke and I might have opened with that but I was told it wasn't original. The truth is, it *was* original, it was original with me, and the fact another person also thought it up is simply a coincidence. I can see why this happened because it's quite an obvious piece of wit.

The famous newspaper tycoon Lord Thompson was in Montreal for a few days — this is the joke here — and when he left a fellow says to his friend: 'I hear Thompson bought the Montreal Star while he was in town."

"What? How much did he pay for it?"

"Ten cents."

I like to pretend I'm creative and a man of great potential. If you have never produced very much in the way of art it's important to believe in your poetential. Observe. I made a typing error and produced a new word, "poetential". By accident I have just described myself perfectly, since I have for some time considered myself a poet and have been meaning for years to write some very good verse.

Generally I'm an accurate speller, that word, as I said, was a slip of the typewriter. Some poets are atrocious spellers. There have always been poor spellers in the world of literature. One day not so long ago I was in the Montreal Public Library reading some books on witchcraft and it was quite a difficult task. I copied down a few passages which will give you an idea of what I mean.

"Alison Peirson was conuict of the vsing of Sorcerie and Witchcraft, with the Inuocation of the spreitis of the Deuill; speciallie in the uisioune and forme of ane Mr. William Sympsoune, hir cousing and moder-brotheris-sone, quha sche affirmit wes ane grit scoller and doctor of medicin...

"The deuell was cled in ane blak goun with ane blak hat upon his head... his faice was terrible, his noise lyk the bek of ane egle, great bournyng eyn; his handis and leggis were herry, with clawes vpon his handis, and feit lyk the griffon."

The author of that must have given his teachers fits while at school. The spelling! There was also a good recipe in the book, used by the witches on special occasions. I don't remember it all but I remember this line: "...a pairt of the head, a pairt of the buttocks, and they made a py thereof..." The husband, as he comes in the door, hollers, "What's for dessert tonight, dear?"

"How abovt ane peece of py?"

I didn't find any answers in witchcraft so I go on daydreaming of extreme and violent deeds to rid the world of its evil.

Living in a city the size of Montreal is no joke. I don't understand how the other citizens tolerate it. But they don't seem to mind. It's the noise that gets me. Well, I realize there are others who are bothered too but we're a minority. It was early in May (of 1963, as I recall), and a man in his undershirt was hammering away fixing his shabby rotten back balcony. Each blow of the hammer was like a cannon going off in a cave, the sound was confined and magnified by the brick walls of the backyards. It was a very hot day, so hot that I couldn't close the windows or I'd suffocate.

The hammering went on. It was like living inside a throbbing toothache or a pounding headache. I got up, paced furiously back and forth, then ran outside. Cars were roaring along the street with horns honking and tires squealing, there were volleys of motorcycles, salvos of heavy trucks, ambulances with sirens screaming. Then thundering above a jet airliner passed over low on its way to landing. When it died away a helicopter appeared, the CJAD traffic helicopter guiding cars to and fro on the city arteries, a head-numbing stuttering clattering of blades. Ah me, sometimes I accommodate myself, I speak to myself and say: "This is the city. When you live in the city this is what you hear. It is not your city, it belongs to others, to those who like it this way. To real city people these sounds are music in their ears, just as the vile air is perfume to their noses, and cement and glass canyons are artistic monuments to man's scope and ingenuity, and crowded sweaty streets display the pride of numbers. All these things are the city. The city is *not* quiet fields where you can hear the wind. It is not little brooks rippling, it is not the fresh scent of pine needles. It is not a sky awash with diamond stars at night, nor the song of crickets, it is not peace and serenity, things do not move leisurely. No, that is the country. So do not confuse the city with the country. If you don't like it here, leave. *But I can't afford to*. Get some money then. Meanwhile, as you are a guest of the city do not try to make it into something it isn't. For one reason, you can't, and trying will only cause frustration and lead to hardening of your arteries and probably insanity. Don't jump when you hear taxis blast their horns for no good reason. You know that in the city taxi drivers operate their cabs with one hand always on the horn. Don't jump and look and say, "Why'd he do that?" and then give him the finger and yell out at him, "Fucking idiot!" so that the city dwellers around you look at you as if you're crazy. The taxi driver doesn't hear you anyway because he's too occupied racing around the streets in a steaming sweat trying to make his eight dollars a day. Montreal has more taxis per population than any other city in North America. If you stand on a downtown street you will find more than half the vehicles that go by are taxis. Seventy-five percent of the horns that are honked are the work of taxi drivers, although there are many, many other drivers who do the same. You could, of course, blame the auto makers who seem to take pains to make horns as loud and nerve-piercing as possible. But then auto makers are city people, and they wouldn't understand if you protested. Protesting only leads to ulcers unless you have the temperament for it. *Some* people could not live happily *without* protesting. They are very valuable members of any community, they are more important than priests, politicians, lawyers, teachers, generals, businessmen, policemen, doctors. They are the most important people of all because they try to check the human animal's boundless and shortsighted rapacity. I mean in particular those who are fighting noise and other man-made products of commerce. They are good and important people. But you, my friend, you aren't one of them.

Hence taking on the job of destroying a city the size of Montreal would be frustratingly impossible, not to say thankless."

So, in summary, my voice's advice was to accept the city while living in it, and leave when I could, but not permit myself to lose my sanity because above all there is one important person in the world and that is me. You may say the same yourself. It is a simple but sad truth and it is why everyone, for instance, is aware that the internal combustion engine causes dangerous problems but very few are willing to give up the one they own. It's really the *other* ones, after all, they should all give up their cars and then there would be only my car, and one car doesn't cause enough contamination to bother a fly.

That hot sunshiny day in May I began to shudder, my stomach sank horribly into a cringing little bladder, my nervous system began to scream, I had not time to go through my rationalizing sermon, to calm myself. I knew I had to get away, if only for a while. I grabbed a train for Quebec City.

§

Quebec is a city, it's true, but it's a much smaller city and its old town is so like old Europe that the mere sight of it is soothing. And a change, wherever you go, is always a balm to the nerves, unless you go some place like jail, which is where I landed shortly, then it's a change for the worse.

Another reason I went to Quebec was I had a friend there, and that meant a place to stay.

When travelling on a train the feel of the wheels, the rhythm of the wheels invariably draws melodies out of me, new melodies never before heard. Someday I'll take a tape recorder with me and hum my melodies into it. Then I'll have proof that I am a musically creative person.

I sat by the window and on the empty seat beside me was my bottle of wine, in a brown paper bag. It was a cheap sherry, called Normandie, but it tasted good, and they make it in New Brunswick — the province I grew up in and possibly the reason I am not a city person and never will be, despite living in places like Montreal and Toronto for various periods. You pay more for the same wine in New Brunswick, but then New Brunswick is a poorer province and there are more winos per capita there. Some day I'll study economics.

It's a pleasure to sit on a train and sip wine. Sometimes you have to compromise with your ideals, unless you're an extreme purist which I am not quite. I used a paper cup, a disposable cup, to drink my wine from, since it would not have looked proper tipping the bottle back, not to mention there was the possibility of the conductor seeing me.

With my shoes off I leaned back and watched the countryside roll by. On a sunny afternoon in May the fields and trees were fresh and vibrantly green. We passed farms with large silos and cows in the fields; we went through little towns, raced through without stopping, French names on the stores, the little balconied hotels, the local taverns, the impressive stone churches. For a while we ran parallel to a highway and I shook my fists at the cars streaming silently along, their noise locked out by the windows of the train and its own clippeting wheels. But I was feeling better, the travelling made me feel better, along with the wine and the sense of escaping from Montreal, and it wasn't long before we pulled into Quebec.

I know there is no other city in North America like Quebec, the old part that is, the walled city and Lower Town. The newer part which sprawls back from the river and up and down is like your average urban mess. And in the old city there are a number of those giant windowed boxes which go under the name of modern city architecture. It amuses me, in an unamusing way, when I look at the Royal Victoria Hospital in Montreal. Half it is old and charming, something like the buildings on the Royal Mile in Edinburgh; in fact it looks like a Scottish castle. The other half was built recently. I picture in my mind the architect saying, when it was decided to build additions to the hospital, standing before the Board of Governors: "I have the perfect design, Gentlemen, a beautiful design, nothing like the ugly antiquated structures you now have. My design, ah, it's breathtaking, the lines, the beauty, it's the height of architectural artistry!" And the governors of course are eager to see a model, but the architect says he forgot to bring it with him. "However, one moment, Gentlemen." And he steps out into the hall and goes to the incinerator room and comes back with a discarded cardboard packing box. "Now." And taking a pen he draws little squares on the sides of the box, identical rows and rows of them, and when finished says: "There. Magnificent! Behold your new buildings." And so they were built and they are there today.

Despite some, as they say, progressive demolition and construction the old city of Quebec still resembles an old city in Europe, it looks much like it did hundreds of years ago when it was built with care and skill, and it has been preserved, buildings restored, conveniences and luxuries added inside but the exteriors kept to the same appearance. The streets are cobblestoned and narrow and rarely follow a straight line. If it weren't for the inevitable congestion of automobiles you could easily walk around the city feeling like an old musketeer.

My friend Bernard lived on Rue Leclerc. He had a large bright room on the second floor of a solid old stone building on the hill. He had a gabled window, and the slanting roof on the street side of his room gave it the appearance of an artist's studio, the traditional attic kind. Bernard was an artist of sorts, he worked with leather. He made belts, sandals, purses, jackets, vests, even pants. In Montreal he had sold his work to boutiques. I myself still wear a wide belt that he made and sold to me. In Quebec, though, he didn't try to do any selling because it would not have been wise, since he was in the act of hiding out from the police.

§

Bernard answered my ring and let me in with a smile. He was almost always smiling, a tiny secret smile as though he knew something that no one else did, and perhaps that was true. I followed him up the narrow flight of stairs to his room. It hadn't been easy to find his place because I was reluctant to ask directions, being not at all fluent in French. And I knew from previous visits to Quebec that English is virtually an unknown language there. I had wandered around a while, reading all the street signs, trying to find it on my own. Once while in Quebec, my first time there, I suffered an embarrassment. Just off the train I went into the first tavern I saw and said to myself, "Now that I'm in Quebec I'm going to act like a Frenchman." So when the waiter came I said, "Une grosse Dow, s'il vous plait." What could be simpler than that? I'd heard it hundreds of times in Montreal taverns. But the waiter, without moving away, said something to me. I hadn't the faintest notion what he was saying, so I repeated, "Grosse Dow, UNB grosse Dow." Then he repeated what he had said, which was gibberish to me. I became slightly flustered, because I knew that he now knew that I had been bluffing, that I couldn't speak French at all. I said "Dow, grosse Dow?" sort of feebly. What had I done wrong? He gave me a look as much as to say I was a stupid ass and went and got me the beer. In a hurry to get out of there I drank it quickly. But before leaving I believe I deduced what he'd been saying. I saw him bring a beer off the shelf rather than out of the cooler to another customer. Thus he must have wanted to know if I preferred my beer cold or off the shelf. Nobody ever asked me that in Montreal.

I stopped a kindly looking old man on the street and said, "Pardon, of est Rue Leclerc?" My pronunciation was very bad because he had me repeat it three or four times. Then his face brightened and he began pouring out the French, none of which I could decipher, and pointing. I said, "Merci," and went off in the direction he'd indicated with his finger. One more such encounter, this time with an attractive girl (since I had to ask somebody), of which there are many in Quebec, brought me to Rue Leclerc and Bernard's address.

Bernard is a tall and athletic looking fellow. In Montreal he had worn an enormous mop of bushy brown hair but for what I assumed to be purposes of disguise it was now trimmed down to where it was almost short. For the same reason he was in the process of growing a moustache.

I respected and admired Bernard, he was a man dedicating his life to a dangerous and important mission, and it had already got him in trouble. About a year ago he had read somewhere, in some radical newspaper it would have been, a letter proposing a scheme for destroying what is sometimes referred to as the car culture. He showed me the letter which he had clipped out. It wasn't long and I can remember the wording more or less. It went like this:

Dear Editor:

What is one of the biggest problems in the North American industrialized consumer-oriented society? The automobile, which kills and maims by collisions and smog, fills the air with noise (as well as fumes), dictates and disfigures the layout of cities and countryside — there is nothing good about it, except its speed which should only be necessary in times of emergency. For transportation subways and electric trains and buses are the answer. Also bicycles. Even a return to horses.

Cars are a perfect object for guerilla attack. Carry a bag of sugar wherever you go and whenever the opportunity arises dump some in the gas tank of a car. Each guerilla should set a goal of a thousand cars knocked out. Fight against the death-dealing and environment disfiguring machine. Exempt only ambulances and fire engines.

Yours for survival,
The Sugar Man

"When I read it," Bernard said to me, 'I realized I'd found what I was looking for. That letter said it all. That was it right there. I'd been casting around, wondering what to do, seeing the world go up in fumes, people thrown out of their low-cost houses to make room for inner city expressways, historical buildings torn down, life becoming a nightmare of engine noises and smells and sights. It was eating me up inside. Yes, that's what it was doing. I had marched in demonstrations, collected petitions, written letters, wore my STOP THE HIGHWAY button. But it didn't help at all, or hardly at all. Then I read that letter and I couldn't get it out of my mind. I knew what I had to do."

So he started doing what the Sugar Man, whoever he might be, advised. He began going about at night and slipping sugar into gas tanks. He made a point of picking out those heavy, powerful racing-type sports cars which a lot of young men affect on the road, the ones with the wide wheels and the huge loud engines and usually with a few decals on them, like "STP" or the Playboy bunny. But if he couldn't find one of these he went for Cadillacs and large Buicks and Oldsmobiles and Chryslers. As a last resort he would knock out a smaller vehicle.

He had gotten to more than a hundred cars when one careless or unlucky night in March he found himself in the glare of a policeman's flashlight. I mentioned that Bernard looked like an athlete but he more than looked it, he was strong and fast, and was able to elude this cop in the dark — after kicking him severely in the groin — and there was quite a hunt on for him, and the story appeared in the papers. Feeling it was the wise thing to do he fled Montreal for Quebec. Unlike myself he could speak some French, enough to get by on satisfactorily.

He called me up one day telling me where he was, asking me to come visit him someday because he knew no one in Quebec. He spent his time working with leather, and also did some metalwork, like making medallions, and he was working on some soapstone carvings as well. He was a tireless, deliberate and talented craftsman and could spend hours at his work and never get bored. But he would like to have some company now and then, he said.

I didn't know for sure that I would make it, but now here I was, for reasons of my own, and he cleared a space on his table and produced two glasses and I poured my wine, of which I had more than half the forty ounce bottle left.

"I have started to keep a journal. A combat log you might call it," said Bernard. We had talked a while, exchanging information; I learned that for the most part he kept to his room, going out occasionally to buy books and groceries and work material. There was a tiny cubbyhole kitchen in his room and he cooked his own meals.

He handed me a thick wirebound notebook. The handwriting was neat, each letter clearly legible, not like my own scrawl which I sometimes can't read myself.

"There's only one entry," he said. 'I started just this morning.' He watched me with his faint and mysterious smile while I read. The date, I believe, was May 12.

I am a General without an army, it began. *There are two kinds of law, the law of the State and the law I follow. These two laws are in contradiction. The law of the State was made in another time and isn't suited to the present age. My law has developed only recently. It is the superior code. I am forced out of conscience to follow it, but it means I must be wary, because in following my law I am breaking the law of the State. Thus when I* sabotage a highway, wreck an automobile or a snowmobile, shoot down a helicopter, bomb an oil company, drive a pulp mill out of business, kidnap a politician, I am doing it in obedience to my own code of ethics and for the good of the earth and all its inhabitants. But should I get caught I will be found guilty by the State because I have contravened its statutes of behaviour. They will accuse me of committing a crime against property or against persons. But I repeat, the State's system of legality is outmoded and serves as a hindrance to the welfare of the earth and its inhabitants rather than a help.

Most people are slow to change their behaviour. You can change their ideas easier but even ideas are very stubborn, the old ideas dig in and give stubborn resistance to the new. Unfortunately there is not time to waste in propagandizing, or should I say proselytizing. By the time sufficient numbers of the public wake up it will be too late. The extent of their unwitting or uncaring destruction will have reached too far, beyond the point of return. There will be a dying giant and nobody around to cure him. He will be too sick to cure himself and barring the unlikely intervention of creatures from another planet that will be the end.

Not everybody is a fool. I am not a fool. I have made my decision to form a guerilla army and fight the machines. Up to now I have been a lone force.

I don't delude myself into thinking I am keeping this record for posterity. The chance of there being a posterity is too remote.

But if I am a casualty before the war is over then it may serve as instruction to others. I will record mistakes as well as correct moves, losses as well as victories. In the event my army is successful — with the aid of similar allied forces which must spring up if we are to win — then this record will serve as a lesson for posterity, and a guide for a better morality than I inherited.

"One man isn't enough," Bernard said, when I was reading. "One man is good but say you want to blow up a factory, something of that size? What's needed is a commando group."

Although he rarely drank much Bernard had bought a large case of beer in the event of having a visitor such as myself, so when the wine was finished our drinking wasn't.

Later we had a lunch of some soup and cheese.

I was thinking, most people reading what Bernard had written in his notebook would consider him a crackpot, a certifiable case. I would have thought that a while back too. Perhaps, in his extremeness, there was an element to him that could be described as fanatical and to some authorities fanaticism is a sickness of the mind. But these are only judgments some people make about others. To my way of thinking, and more so to Bernard's, the condition of the earth was extreme and had been brought on by fanatical human greed and stupidity. An extreme condition generally needs an extreme cure. You don't treat a diseased appendix with an aspirin, you attack it with a knife, you cut it out, you destroy it. If there were no disease then to cut a man open with a knife would appear fanatical. It depends on how you look at things.

Bernard drank three or four beers of the two dozen in the case, and around midnight he became sleepy. Aside from the effect of this unaccustomed drinking he was in the habit of going to bed quite early.

But I wasn't tired. I always stayed up late at night and drinking was nothing new to me. In fact I had, and still have, an unmistakable partiality to it. Sometimes, however, particularly when talking to someone, I tend to overdo it. This was one of those times. I don't know how many beers I had, I know I had most of the forty ounces of wine. I had over a dozen pints, and shortly after Bernard went to sleep I reeled out into the street looking for something to do, for I felt the night was still in its youth. My memory gets a little vague around this point. I have elusive visions of various bars. I know I must have returned to Bernard's at one point, because where else could I have gotten the sugar?

The Crime

It wasn't even a particularly dark street, there were streetlights and store windows with their night lights on, and several cars drove by, and there were people passing on the sidewalk. Some of them stopped to watch me. I was holding the bag of sugar and laughing out loud, a kind of hysterical chuckling. I kept thinking what I'd tell Bernard in the morning. The people and the moving cars were like shadows in the dark, spirit things, I paid them no attention at all. Tottering, stumbling to regain my balance, I found the cap to the gas tank of a car, fumbled it off, tipped the bag of sugar. It was a messy job, the sugar poured everywhere. I thought I must have enough in there. It struck me that I didn't know how much sugar you had to use. But that must be plenty, I thought. I tried to put the cap back on but it wouldn't go, I couldn't find the threads. I tossed it away, then moved to the next car. I don't recall how many cars I treated, probably only two or three because of my drunken awkwardness. They may have told me later, if they ever found out exactly, but I wasn't in very good condition for listening. There were policemen standing beside me. I was driving in a police car to the station.

"Occupation?"

"Poet." I thought that was a clever thing to say. The cop at the desk wrote it down.

They asked me many questions. I must not mention Bernard, my brain was saying to itself. Although I remember very little it doesn't mean I was unable to think and to retain some cunning and responsibility at the same time. My mind is now virtually blank about that night, but it was not blank then.

If I had no place to stay where did I intend to sleep, they wanted to know. I was seated by a desk and there were detectives facing me.

I was going to spend the night at the train station and then leave for Montreal in the morning, I said.

Where did I get the sugar?

I bought it in a supermarket.

Why was I putting it in gas tanks?

I was going to siphon the gas out and in case I swallowed some I preferred it with sugar.

I don't know if it was that answer or others I made like it, but suddenly a great meaty hand whapped me across the face. My head rang. One of the detectives was swearing at me. They threw me in a cell and I went to sleep.

§

Sometime in the morning I awoke. I saw the bars when I opened my eyes and I tried to orient myself, to remember what happened. I had a terrible pounding headache, I lay there in a heap of nausea. Then it came to me, vague and sickening memories of cars and sugar and lights and policemen.

§

Do you know what you're here for?" said a voice through the bars.

"I've got an idea what for," I said, sitting on the hard bunk, head in hands.

The Trial

"This is a most unusual case. You are charged with the deliberate destruction of private property, wanton destruction it would appear..." The Magistrate had an intelligent and it seemed to me even a kind face. He looked like the fatherly, compassionate, wise sort of man you would ideally assign the god-like position of Magistrate, arbiter among men in matters of life and death, freedom and captivity — those most important conditions of the human body and spirit. He was about sixty with greying hair. His face was calm and thoughtful, eyes alive, curious, probing.

You run across reports in the newspapers of judges who are filled with hate, who pass sentence by the measuring rod of their prejudices, whether they involve youth, politics, race, religion, costume, sex, social status, comportment. Judges as a rule are dangerous men and it's a bad thing indeed to run afoul of them. For instance, if someone were to insult you to your face, call you a moron or a lackey or a hypocrite, and this person is younger and stronger than you, and say his accusations are true — Naturally you don't want to be called these things, even if they are true, but what can you do? With most of us, we can burn up inside and conjure in our minds horrible fantasies of vengeance. But if you're a judge on the bench you can say, "Six months in jail for saying that."

But there's a flaw in the magistrate's power. Almost certainly he has never been a prisoner in jail, thus he's not fully able to savour what he's doing to a man when he sends him there. If he understood what six months in jail was like, well, it would be just as satisfying sentencing a man to six *days*—knowing what it's like—as six months or six years when you don't have a proper appreciation of what you're doing.

It's like the difference between playing poker with real money or with match sticks.

Judges, as some observers have suggested, should for their own benefit undergo a week in prison before taking to the bench. It has been done in the past by a few extraordinary jurists, and can be accomplished quite easily using an assumed run-of-the-mill offence like car theft or embezzlement.

I sensed my judge was not typical when he said "it would appear" that I had wantonly destroyed the automobiles, or attempted to. He was curious about me.

I stood just inside the door of a large room. It was more like a private study than a courtroom. The Magistrate sat behind an enormous elevated desk in the furthest corner of the room. Along the dark panelled walls were bookshelves with glass doors. There were several padded-leather chairs. The ceiling was high, the floor was shiny with polished gray tiles. There were three tall windows with heavy drapes on them.

My companion, my guard, whatever he was, a small man wearing glasses who had escorted me from the cell, stood a little behind me. With the Magistrate were two young lawyers, one casually half-sitting against the desk, arms folded, the other standing with hands in his pockets. Like the Magistrate they eyed me with interest, showing no signs of animosity. They wore well-fitting suits and vests, jackets casually unbuttoned. I might remark that I myself was bearded and wearing denim pants, cowboy boots and an old sweatshirt with a KILL CARS button pinned on my chest. I had thought of removing the button, which by the way was one of Bernard's creations, since it kind of gave me away, but decided there was no point doing so since the cops would have already noted it in their report.

After the Magistrate read the formal charge against me, he said: "How do you plead, guilty or not guilty?"

"What happens if I plead not guilty?" I said, my voice sounding the way I felt, anaemic.

"You can have your trial postponed and in the meantime get yourself a lawyer."

"I don't have money to pay a lawyer," I said. More than that, the thought of waiting in anxiety for a future trial did not sit well with me. I wanted to have done with this. I thought I would be found guilty in any case, having been caught redhanded with at least twenty witnesses on the scene.

The Magistrate waited.

"I guess I'll have to plead guilty," I said, "but I'm not guilty."

"You're not? Weren't you caught putting sugar in the gas tanks of cars?"

"Well... I suppose I was. But you're asking me if I'm guilty of a crime and you're prepared to sentence me to punishment. But the owners of those cars and the men who made them and everyone who profited off them, the dealers, the insurance companies, the garage owners, they're guilty of a crime against the natural earth and everything that lives on the earth. I'm not the guilty person. Why should I be punished?" I had a hard time getting this out, I stumbled a bit and stuttered over a few words and did not sound forceful because I was physically incapable of any kind of force, being on the verge of collapsing. The combination of a severe hangover and my unhappy predicament had squeezed most of the stamina out of me. However my mind felt sharp enough. And somewhat to my surprise I wasn't intimidated, I wasn't overwhelmed by the Magistrate and his courtroom. It may have been the alcohol still in my blood; it may have been a courage born out of pure misery.

The Judge and the lawyers whispered together. They were far enough away in that big room that I couldn't hear anything they said.

"Do you think that's the way to cure a problem—and we all realize there's a problem with the automobile and pollution—by taking the law into your own hands?"

"Well..." I was reluctant to say yes. There was a limit to how far I could go. I am not made in a heroic mould. Something cunning in me spoke in my ear, saying: "If he thinks you're repentant he'll become sympathetic and might let you off."

"Laws are being enacted to fight pollution," the Judge said. 'I will tell you something of my own experience. I have a house in the country and last winter I had a lot of trouble with snowmobiles. I don't have to tell you about those machines, the noise they make, the many cases of trespassing and destruction of property, the mess their drivers leave behind. Now I became very angry about them. But I didn't go and break the law and attack them myself. I worked with the law, not against it. I brought several offenders to court and had them charged with trespassing and disturbing the peace. They were fined and taught a lesson."

If I had not been in the situation I was in, I would have loved to ask the Magistrate how much they were fined, if they still owned and operated their vehicles (away from his property, of course), if they realized what a real problem they were, if it encouraged other owners of such machines to give them up... Many things I could have asked. I could have mentioned that a Minister of the Quebec Government, the Transport Minister who was responsible for the regulating of all vehicles including snowmobiles, himself owned four of them, one for each member of his family. And the Federal Government subsidized companies that made the machines, to the tune of several million dollars each year.

But I didn't say any of this, because the last thing I wanted was an argument. What I did want was a suspended sentence. Or a small fine. Or one day in jail. I wanted to get the hell out of there and on the streets and far away.

"I think that's a very good thing you did," I said, "and if more people reacted the same way perhaps something could be done about environment problems. But too many don't care. And I was very drunk last night. I was visiting the city and got carried away and got so drunk I can hardly remember what happened and when I heard cars screeching by and honking horns and leaving blue smoke behind them something must have happened to me. That's the only way I can explain it. So you see, in one way I'm guilty, but I'm not really, because I was drunk and not in control of myself, and on top of that I was doing something which the Government should be doing. I was trying to improve our environment."

The Magistrate and the two young lawyers whispered some more.

Then the Magistrate looked at me for a while. He said finally: "It's obvious you're an intelligent young man, and I don't believe that at heart you're a criminal. But there is a law, and without this law none of us would have any degree of security. For example, a certain man might decide he needs those boots you're wearing more than you do because his feet are sore and he has five children to support. If there were no law, if he followed his own law, he would be justified in his own eyes in taking those boots from you even if it meant injuring or even killing you to get them." He waited a moment for that to sink in. It didn't convince me in the least, but I nodded my head.

"You understand?"

"I can see what you mean." But it's not the same thing, I said to myself. Because I don't even step on ants with my boots, they don't hurt anyone.

"How do you plead?" he said.

"Well, I guess I plead guilty," I said.

"You don't have to plead guilty, as I've told you."

I shrugged, and didn't say anything else.

"I'll have to sentence you, then," he said, "since that's your plea. I see you have no previous record; and clearly drunkenness influenced your actions, although it's no excuse before the law. The people who own those cars will naturally be very angry. I can't let you off entirely. The best I can do is give you a short time in jail. I sentence you to two weeks in jail. They'll feed you well there and you won't have to worry about a place to sleep for a few days." I had told the police earlier when they questioned me that I had no job in Montreal, and had been staying with different friends; I was a poet, I said, and it was tough making ends meet. I made a point of mentioning that I'd done three years at university though I'd found no use for it insofar as employment went. I think my education, common as it is today, didn't hurt me with the Magistrate. It enabled him to accept me as an idealist and not as a common vandal. I was told later by others that had I gotten a different sort of judge, and most of them were different, I would have been lucky to escape with six months. To many persons an automobile is still a sacred thing.

As for going to jail, I told myself however unconvincingly that it would be a valuable experience, something worth having in my past.

Led Off To Gaol

I was taken to a room in the basement of the police station where a smiling man with thinning blonde hair photographed me front and side with a number beneath my mug—like a genuine criminal. Then I was told to stand on a scale and weigh myself, then my height was measured, and finally, holding my hand the way you teach a child to write, the blonde man rolled each of my fingers separately on an ink pad, then rolled it again on my identification form, thus fingerprinting me.

After that I was kept in a cell until a guard came for me and I was taken to a room where there were other prisoners, newly sentenced, still wearing their civilian clothes. We were handcuffed together in pairs and loaded into a van and driven through the streets of Quebec to the *Prison de Quebec* on the Plains of Abraham. There were seven other prisoners besides myself, all men in their twenties, all French, and they seemed to be in high spirits as though this was an old and not unpleasant routine to them. They laughed and joked with each other and when we passed a pretty girl on the street they waved and shouted at her through the barred window of the van. I was not able to put up such a front, the best I could do was grin weakly.

The van pulled up at the door of a huge old greystone building with barred windows and a high wall around it. We were herded inside, our handcuffs were removed, then we were led straight to a mess hall for a bite to eat. It was a large room with three long rows of picnic-style tables with benches attached. We lined up at a small window giving onto the kitchen and were handed each a tray of food. This particular tray held soup, bread, sausages, a scoop of potatoes and green beans, not bad if you were in any way hungry. When we were seated an inmate came around with a huge pail of coffee and ladled it into enamel cups. Our only eating utensil was a tablespoon (it was like this at all meals, I soon learned) so you had to butter your bread with the spoon as well as cut your meat and stir your coffee. I ate a little bread and soup and drank some coffee but I was far from having an appetite.

After the meal we were ushered away to be processed into the prison. I was told to hand over whatever I had in my pockets. As usual, as happened at every turn I took, and as was to be expected, I was spoken to in French and had to mumble, "Sorry I don't understand French." I was half afraid I'd be cursed at as a "maudit anglais!" and kicked in the head but it never happened. Instead they spoke to me in English and with no animosity that I could see.

My valuables consisted of a wallet with twelve dollars in it, a bit of change, the keys to my little apartment back in Montreal, and a slightly used handkerchief. These items were placed in an envelope and I signed a paper which listed them.

While counting my money, the officer said, "How come you put sugar in those gas tanks?"

"I was drunk," I said.

He shook his head, mystified.

In another room I had to strip and take a shower. Then I was given my jail costume of a baggy pair of gray cotton pants with no front pockets, a shirt of the same colour and material, a pair of undershorts and an undershirt, gray woolen socks and old black army boots. They also gave me a towel which every inmate carried around with him, in most cases folded up in a little ball in his back pocket. Once dressed I was taken through a series of barred doors which were locked behind me and at the end of the journey deposited in a large ground-level room with a crowd of other men. A heavy metal door with a small barred peephole in it slammed shut behind me.

I found myself in the midst of a wrestling match. A number of heads turned to look me over and there were some shouted comments and hoots of laughter thrown my way, probably because of my beard. Not understanding a word I replied with my sickly grin and sidled along the wall and leaned against it, trying my best to become invisible.

There was a lot of hollering and thrashing about as the two wrestlers, one a boy around eighteen with the build of a bulldog, and the other a middle-aged man with a great paunch on him, rolled and flopped around on the cement floor. There was no end of grunting and groaning and punching and stomping, in the burlesque style of professional wrestling, and there was only a little seriousness in it all, enough to frighten me.

I decided to have a look around. I hadn't lost all my shakiness but my headache had left me and I didn't feel I was going to throw up anymore.

There wasn't much to look at. Besides the room I was in there were two others of similar size connecting with it by open doorways. Along the walls were benches. In one room there were three rough picnic tables. Through barred windows you looked out on the prison yard and stone walls which must have been forty feet high. There was nothing in the yard but a paved surface. There was nothing in the common rooms but a few benches. It was a very simple prison. I soon found out there was nothing much to do here but wait. There were two segregated wings, the one I was in where sentences ranged up to six months, and a wing for those doing longer stretches. I later saw the long-termers out the window. On days when an outdoor exercise period was permitted they did their pacing or sitting in the yard at a different time from ours.

There were two toilets in the common rooms. They stood on a slightly elevated part of the floor in compartments with no doors, and the bowls had no seats. When I strolled by a man was sitting there with his pants down around his ankles having a crap. You either had to shit in public or keep it to yourself.

My stroll didn't last long because it took but a minute to see what was to be seen. There were some two hundred men in the three rooms, some sitting on the benches, some pacing slowly and methodically, several standing talking together. At the moment a few dozen were watching the wrestling match near the entrance. I discovered before long that of these two hundred men I was the only English-speaking one among them, although some of them were able to speak one form of English or another along with their native French.

I noticed someone was talking to me, though for a moment I wasn't sure he meant me. It was the paunchy man I'd seen wrestling. He handed me a crumpled package about a third filled with tobacco. Stuck in with the tobacco were some papers.

"For me? Thanks. *Merci*," I said. I couldn't understand why he was giving me tobacco. I had quit smoking cigarettes about a year before but I had a suspicion I was going to start again with a lot of time on my hands, so I accepted the tobacco. Was it because I looked so lost, I wondered? Later I found out it was the custom, tradition or whatever to give each newcomer a bit of tobacco as a welcoming gesture. The fat man, I learned, was the trusty, and it was to him you went when you needed toilet paper. He handed out little rolls with no cardboard cylinder in the middle, they were fashioned by him, probably four or five out of a regular roll of paper. You carried your toilet paper in one back pocket and your towel in the other.

At five o'clock we had supper. The food wasn't bad, better than you'd expect considering the dismalness of the place. But I still wasn't hungry and ate only a few spoonfuls.

At six o'clock we were marched two-by-two to our cells. I was grateful for that because I'd been feeling nervous and uncomfortable. I was anxious to get by myself. The lone English-speaking person among two hundred French Canadians, still trembling inside from the drunkenness of the previous night and the experiences since morning, not knowing what was coming next—under the circumstances the privacy of a cell was welcome.

I was taken to a cell block two levels high and placed in a line at the top level before one of the narrow barred doors. A sergeant with a thick ginger moustache came along with two guards, and holding a clipboard before him checked off our names. Then we disappeared into our respective cells and a guard passed along the corridor slamming the heavy metal locks shut. Other guards were performing the same duty in other corridors and the sounds clanked and echoed off the walls.

It was still bright out and across from my door was a tall barred window. We were in an upper part of the building and through the window I was able to see over the great wall outside and across the Saint Lawrence River where the hills and trees and tiny houses and a silver-roofed church looked very peaceful. It seemed very far from where I was, a pointedly different sort of world. Despite telling myself I was only to be here two weeks I felt lonely and hopeless as hell.

Once you stepped into your cell you were on a narrow bed. The space was so small that the bed touched the walls on both sides and at the far end, and at the cell entrance there was a space of one foot, and most of this was taken up by a bucket-sized tin can which gave off a strong smell of disinfectant. This was the toilet. To give you an idea how narrow my quarters were, when I lay on my back I could put my two forefingers together and touch both walls with my elbows. When it got dark I learned that the only light available was what came through the bars from the dusky corridor. By the prison routine all inmates were locked in their cells from six in the evening until six in the morning.

I hardly have to say I felt very little romance about my situation. As a youngster I imagined that being in jail was somehow a romantic experience, no doubt because of the influence of various novels and movies. Now, with night coming on, that desolate twilight time, other inmates yelling and swearing and singing, a few transistor radios turned up full blast, filthy whitewashed rough stone walls beside me, I felt like a hapless orphan. I told myself it was a good thing I wasn't facing a six-month sentence, the despair would be unbearable. I had a pencil with me, they let me keep my pencil and a little notebook I carried, and I debated marking up a "1" on the wall, because I'd almost completed one day of the fourteen. But it seemed more logical to put the mark there the following morning. I had a few matches, I'd found a card with a couple in it stuck in with the tobacco, and I rolled a cigarette. Later I rolled another one, then another one, using up the last match, and after that I chain-smoked. It wasn't until the next day I learned to split my paper matches in two, something I should have thought of myself. Smoking was a slight comfort, though it made me dizzy after such a long period of abstinence. The evening dragged on slowly. I had my thoughts, my tobacco, and two weeks to wait. As anyone knows, nothing makes time drag like waiting.

I realize there are those who would accept my situation with a shrug, say what the hell, I might as well be here as in Iceland. But I suspect I am more of a coward and a weakling than many others. Consequently being where I was depressed me. I'll confess that when I crawled under my rough woolen blankets I was on the point of tears. I usually sleep without a pillow, but when I shoved aside the lumpy pillow on my bed and lay my face on the mattress cover I was met by a revolting smell of vomit. I retained the pillow after that.

To help put myself to sleep, to try and find some comfort, I reverted to an old practice of my younger days; I started saying the Rosary on my fingers. Was I still a believer? It didn't really matter. I had no scruples about using my old friend the Virgin Mary for a night even if I was a heretic or agnostic or whatever. It was comforting, in any case, and I drifted off to sleep sometime during the third decade of Hail Mary's. I was able to make it through the subsequent nights on my own.

§

I was awakened in the gray of the morning by a guard opening the cell doors with his big iron key. My sleeping mind had stayed alert to where I was so waking was not a shock. The guard had gone past my door and I noticed it was open a few inches. I put my clothes on and sat on the bed and waited. Nobody had told me what I was to do. Then I saw some other inmates going by carrying their pails so I picked up mine and followed them.

In a washing room with rows of sinks there were two toilets against the wall and I stood in line at one of these, because that's what everybody else was doing. I saw they were dumping their buckets. When it came my turn I dumped mine, though there was nothing in it but some liquid disinfectant, then rinsed it out in a sink as the men before me were doing. I thought I would have to keep alert and watchful so that I could learn what I was supposed to do. It didn't appear anyone was going to instruct me. I splashed some water on my face and picked up my bucket and followed the flow of listless men back to the cells.

There was a few minutes of hanging around near the washroom after that, until we were lined up and paraded down to breakfast. As each man finished eating he got up and went to the common rooms. I was let in through the steel door and it was locked behind me. I spent a day of sitting, pacing, smoking. You could smoke in the common rooms without wasting matches, because on one of the walls there was an electrical contraption that served as a lighter. You pressed a button and it made a buzzing and sparkling sound and a jagged thread of fire danced between two circuits. It looked like a miniature version of something out of a mad scientist's laboratory.

There were men of all ages in the prison, but most of them were old beaten looking guys, derelicts in for drunkenness. At that time in Quebec, I don't know if it's the same now, there was a law that graduated the jail terms for drunkenness convictions. The first time you got a sentence of a week, the second time a month or so, and the third time and every time after that you got six months—unless you could pay a substantial fine, of course. During those six months a man was confined half the time to a tiny cell, and the other half he spent in three connected rooms like three cement boxes with a large number of other men and nothing to do besides pace the floor or sit and stare into space. Some of the men I saw looked like zombies, pacing slowly along the walls, stopping a moment when face to a wall, turning around methodically and retracing their steps, passing by each other like slow drifting ghosts.

Those of the inmates who had money could buy tobacco; the others did without or bummed what they could. A lot of the older men had spent a great deal of time in the prison for drunkenness. They would serve their six months, get out, and inevitably be picked up drunk and have to serve another six months.

Some days, if the weather was good, the inmates were permitted to go out in the yard for two hours in the afternoon. But out there, although you had the fresh air, the scene was more of the same: men pacing, men sitting in abstracted silence, some men talking in groups, some of the younger ones exploding their energy by wrestling and fooling around.

Now and then someone would say something to me in French, but I had to give them an apologetic look and say I spoke English. A few of the young guys asked me what I was in for. They were able to speak a little English.

"Stealing a car," I said.

"What did dey give you, 'ow much time?"

"Two weeks."

"Two weeks!"

"Yeah."

"You were very lucky. It could 'ave been at leas' two month."

"Yeah. I guess I got a good judge."

That day, my first full day there, was the longest I've ever had to put in in my entire young life. I was wearing a watch and I couldn't keep from looking at it every so often, waiting for my sentence to get over with. As short as two weeks seems, when five minutes takes two hours to go by, two weeks is like an awful long time.

Fortunately I was able to buy tobacco and matches. The bit I was given didn't last long. It happened to be the right day for it because supplies were sold only twice a week. I smoked and smoked until my mouth was raw. The hours were divided into innumerable cigarettes. If you did nothing at all, if there was no sequence of events, no markers along the way, it was like being trapped in eternity. I shoved minutes behind me with cigarettes. The thought of six months of such days, which was the prospect for many of the others, was almost beyond my comprehension.

When six o'clock finally dragged around I was again eager for my cell. So many people surrounding me in the close quarters of the common rooms put my nerves on edge. Having never thought of myself as a convict I felt sorely out of place among the others who were plainly experienced, perhaps even natural prisoners. I was afraid they might find me out for what I was. Should they learn I was a mistake, not a criminal at all, that the clothes I was wearing were a masquerade, there was no telling what might happen. I avoided looking at anyone, I paced as others did, slow and dreamy; I sat on the rough benches with a vacant look on my face (so I imagined). I pretended to be deep in my thoughts and waiting out my time. I tried to be a part of the background. When someone spoke to me it terrified me. I was fearful of giving myself away. It seemed to me the others were here because it was their way of life and I was an outsider who had stumbled by sheer accident in among them. I felt like a lamb in wolf's clothing.

In my cell I was able to relax somewhat. Time dragged there just as slowly but my locked door gave me a sense of safety. I had not had a shit in over two days, and though I'd felt an impulse to during the day I resisted it rather than sit on a toilet in plain view of two hundred men. I know this is an unnecessary inhibition, but I have it and it's very hard to put aside. Now, in my cell, I thought, if I feel the urge I have my own little can. But that was not easy either. For one thing, the cells were close together and with barred doors not being exactly soundproof you could hear men along the corridor coughing, burping, farting, blowing noses, even breathing. When someone was on the can you knew it. That meant they could hear me too. But, I told myself, they won't know it's me because they can't see me. Maybe the two guys on each side of me and the fellow up above would know, but that's all. And they couldn't be sure. But it still inhibited me when I was on the can. Worse than that, the guards often came strolling by and the can was wedged between the head of the bed and the bars, so you would be only inches from the guard and in plain view of him if he came by. Moreover it was very cramped and sitting on a tin can is no pleasure. I was constipated for something like four or five days. After that I attempted a few craps on the stage downstairs and others with more success on my own personal can.

§

75

The following day I discovered there was a library in the prison, and that the inmates had the privilege of borrowing two books a week.

"Dey 'ave da h'English book too," one of the inmates told me. He had been kind enough to inform me that it was this afternoon that you could go to the library, the one afternoon of the week it was open.

I have always been a big reader of books but I never wanted a book to read as badly as I did then. From the library, a one-room establishment but quite heavily stocked, I took out *The Grapes of Wrath* and *The Good Earth*. They were pocket books and were protected by brown paper covers. Clutching them like bags of gold I sat at one of the picnic tables in the south room (the three connecting rooms formed an L) and flipped through the pages, then looked out the window facing me at one of the walls, then took a pleasurefully long time deciding which book to begin first. There was no rush about making up my mind, nor was there about reading when I started. I decided on Steinbeck's first since I'd meant for some time to read *The Grapes of Wrath*. I read the first paragraph, and read it again, examining each word carefully before proceeding to the next paragraph. I was indeed a grateful man. Not only had I something to read which would help me put the time in, but it would be obvious to the other inmates that I was busy reading and not in need of someone to talk to. There were quite a few other men with their noses in books, and later on I noticed they traded amongst themselves, something I couldn't do because I had the only English books. But I observed too that a good many of the men didn't bother to get books; the zombies continued their perpetual slow marches, or their vacant-eyed vigils on the benches; the younger fellows were too busy gabbing or shoving each other around; and probably there were men who couldn't read.

When I finished two pages I closed the book and got up and paced around the room for a while, in order to alternate my activities, all two of them. When I'd done about ten minutes of walking I sat down again and very slowly and deliberately resumed reading, sometimes going over the same lines three or four times. There was a perceptible movement of time. I felt that I had been partially rescued from my sentence. I believed now I could get through the remaining days. Before I'd had my doubts, I was afraid I might suddenly start crumbling into little pieces.

Despite my attempts at invisibility—let me say this once more, perhaps I can get it straight—I was periodically spoken to in a string of unintelligible French, and it was, as I've mentioned, embarrassing to interrupt and mumble I couldn't understand. Whoever was talking to me either left it at that and walked away, or he stayed to talk with whatever English he possessed. When that happened I had to play a part and for me that is very difficult. I had to lie about my crime. I said I stole a car. I didn't dare tell the truth because I was quite sure I would not be understood. That's the problem, you see, when you're doing someone a favour and he can't see where it's a favour, in fact it might well look like an affront, an injury to him. I wouldn't want anyone to do *me* such a favour, like burn my house down so I could experience the joy of sleeping under the open sky. Sabotaging the modern world was a ticklish assignment to give yourself because it was easy to see where such a moral decision was open to abuse, where any nut could try and shape the world his way despite the victims he might leave behind in doing it. But that's the way it goes. You have to act by your own lights.

Probably none of the men in with me owned a car. But probably every one of them would like to. Stealing a car then was understandable, a realistic thing to do. Destroying cars had to be the work of a madman.

§

When we were getting ready to parade up to our cells that evening one of the men said to me, "Dere's anodder guy speaks h'English 'ere, 'e got 'ere dis afternoon, 'e wants to see you. I'll show you 'im tomorrow."

While waiting to go down to breakfast next morning a slightly-built man with a tanned face and a neat moustache appeared at my elbow. "Am I glad to see you, I thought I'd go nuts in here," he said. 'I can't make out what these gazoonies are saying at all, can you?"

His name was Dan Kiley, he said. He was in his mid-forties and looked a bit like a smaller-sized, down-and-out version of Clark Gable. Because of him

I never got around to reading *The Good Earth*. I had made a start on *The Grapes of Wrath* and managed to finish that book by reading in the dim light of my cell, but during the day I was content enough to listen to Dan tell stories.

For want of a better way of doing this I will give him a chapter to himself, since I didn't say all that much myself but mostly listened. The appearance of the days were the same, sitting on a bench indoors, or on the hard pavement in the yard leaning back against the wall in the sun, smoking steadily, Dan talking, me listening. It made the time pass very well.

Dan Tells Some Stories

Riding the Rails

"I wouldn't be here talking to you now if I hadn't done something stupid," he said, the first time we sat down to talk. "I hope it taught me a lesson, but I doubt it. I'm a traveller, you understand. Travelling is my profession, I'm always travelling, but I *never* go by train, it would make no sense. Only in a moment of foolishness would I take a train. In my business I have to stop at as many towns as possible, and when I'm on the road I can usually, if you'll pardon the expression, put the bum on whoever picks me up. But as sometimes happens, and it happens as often as possible, I was a bit intoxicated yesterday and found myself beside a railroad track just outside this very city. I don't know what I was doing there, I think the track happened to be beside the highway, and as I sat on the grass passing the time a line of boxcars came slowly by with the doors open. Whatever possessed me I couldn't say, but I climbed into a car. It went for a few hundred yards and then stopped. Then it began backing up. Then it started forward again and stopped once more. This train, I thought, is not going anywhere, so I decided to disembark. When my feet touched ground I felt a big hand on my collar. It belonged to a railroad cop.

"This morning I said to the judge, 'Your Honour, I am travelling to New Brunswick to work in the woods, and being in financial distress at present that was the only train I could afford to ride. I am sure you can sympathize with a man when he's hard up, the state of the economy in the country being what it is.'

"He was a miserable looking old bastard. He looked down his long nose at me and said, 'Thirty days! Next.'

"I admit I'm a little concerned about being in here, you see there's a warrant out for my arrest in Vancouver. But I doubt if they'll transport me all the way out there. It was a mere ten dollar cheque and for ten dollars I can't see them going to the expense of sending me with an escort all the way to Vancouver. That, also, was a foolish thing for me to do, cashing that cheque. But a man does some foolish things under the influence of drink. It was a particularly bad act because in my past there's a little matter of two years where I was a guest at Kingston Penitentiary because of writing cheques. They wouldn't hesitate to give me the same or more on a similar charge."

His Beginnings

"You know, my father was a band leader in Windsor, it was a dance band, and for a while I played clarinet with him. Then he died and I got married and next thing I found myself owning a little farm away out in the sticks. That may sound strange when you look at me now, but at the time it seemed the type of life I wanted, the landed gentry sort of thing. When I was a kid I'd spent summers on a farm with my grandparents and that left many happy memories. But after five years of trying to make a living farming I figured I'd worked enough to last me the rest of my life. I said to my wife, goodbye, you can have everything that's here, for what it's worth—and I left. And I've been on the bum ever since. That was twenty years ago. I'm an unrepentant alcoholic and a bum and I wouldn't be anything else. I'm one of the few free men in this country. So I'm in jail now, but this is a resting place, an oasis. I'll be off the booze while I'm here and I'll eat well and leave healthy as a horse. There's one thing about me, unlike other winos, as the public refers to us, and that is I can eat. Most of the others never eat and that's why they come to grief."

The Great Northern Mining Co.

"I figured even if I was a bum there was no point living like one. I got hold of a few dollars and bought some sharp looking clothes. I earned the money. I worked occasionally in those days, I painted, cooked, I was a salesman different times, but never long at anything because it was never long before I'd hit the bottle—and then invariably I lost my interest in being employed, particularly since I'd be fired by then for being drunk on the job or not showing up for work. Anyway, as little work as I did I felt it was too much, and on top of that I felt I was living beneath my station. As an intelligent man of cultivated tastes I wasn't content sheltering in Sally Anns with a lot of deadbeats. With my talents I knew I could do better. And I did. I got hold of a new suit, got some business cards printed up: John Davidson, Vice-President, Great Northern Mining Company, Sudbury, Ont., very official looking. Then I went travelling for the company, staying at posh hotels, cashing cheques, buying more expensive clothes and luggage, laying out big tips, drinking the best booze. That was the life I'd been designed for. I got more business cards made with different companies and different pseudonyms so I wouldn't leave too clear a trail behind me. Of course business cards and expensive clothes aren't enough to make the full impression, you need the right mannerisms, the correct attitude. When you walk into a hotel you've got to look like you own the place. If you fit the part nobody's going to want to offend you by demanding excessive proof that you are who you say you are.

"Except sometimes I'd run into a desk clerk or a manager who must have been burned before. I remember once I tried to pay my bill with a cheque and the clerk balked and called the manager.[1] The manager said they didn't take personal cheques unless, and he was very polite about it, they were perfectly satisfied with the identity of the guest. My story apparently didn't satisfy him. I gave him a difficult time about it but I knew by the stubborn look in his eye that I was going to have some trouble. In fact the more I talked the more suspicious he became. Finally he said, 'I'm afraid I'm going to have to call the police and have them check things out. If your story is true, and I'm sure it is, we'll owe you a deep apology. I would like to accept your cheque and personally I would, but I can't go against hotel policy.' Well, what could I do? I couldn't pay the bill, I had only ten dollars in my pocket. And I couldn't run, because the manager was a giant of a man and the clerk was there as well, and there were husky bellhops hanging around. I'd never have made it to the door. And besides, that wasn't my style. I said, 'By all means call the police. I'd like nothing better, anything to clear this matter up. I've never been treated in such a deplorable manner before, I assure you,' and so on. I was highly

---

[1] This was in the days before credit cards.

indignant. Pretty soon a detective arrived and I immediately said, 'Good day, sir, I'm glad you got here, my name is Davidson of the Great Northern Mining Company, and I'm having a deuce of a time with this gentleman here.' I immediately took the initiative, I handed him my card and began complaining about the treatment I was getting. 'What kind of fool would carry a couple of hundred dollars around in his pocket?' I said, for I owed the hotel a hundred and eighty. 'What in hell were cheques invented for if you can't use them?' After I'd finished my spiel the detective looked at the manager and said, 'Well?'

"The manager was not a hundred per cent sure of himself, not by any means. Remember, I didn't look like a bum or anything, you could see my luggage was good quality, and I was putting on a good performance of an indignant executive. 'I'm really sorry to cause this trouble,' he said, 'but our hotel has lost money over bad cheques in the past and lately we've been taking no chances. Believe me, it's nothing personal, I quite willingly accept your story but I can't ignore the policy.'

"'Look,' the detective said, and I could see he tended to believe my line, just by the way he acted, 'we can settle this very easy. It's just a matter of making a quick call to Mr. Davidson's company and verifying his identity.'

"'Of course, of course,' said the hotel manager. 'It's really no trouble at all, anything to clear this unfortunate business up. Naturally the hotel will pay for the call.' Now, you can imagine how that made me feel. They both turned to me and I thought, well, what can I do, I might as well say, 'Okay, you've got me, I throw in the towel.' But what the hell, experience has taught me that it's always best to hang in there until the final bell, a few more minutes wouldn't hurt, so I decided to bluff through to the bitter end. I had nothing to lose. The company I used on my card was a real company, by the way. A phony one could be checked out by simply looking in a telephone book. I said, 'Very well, if you refuse to take my word for it, if you insist on treating me like some sort of criminal... by all means call my head office.' The manager, who I noticed was getting more uneasy the longer this went on, said, 'No, no, it's not like that at all, it's merely a standard precaution, I certainly do accept your word, Mr. Davidson.' But he didn't offer to forget about the phone call.

"The manager asked the switchboard to put the call through and the detective took the phone. I was in a sweat, at least internally. On the surface I was careful to keep my composure. For what reason, I'll never really know. My heart was down in my shoes, the show was going to be over any second now. 'What? What's that you say?' the cop was saying into the phone. 'Nobody there? Goddammit. That's right, so it is. I never thought about that.' He hung up. 'Their offices are closed today, it's the Labor Day weekend.' He looked like he thought he'd been made a fool of. 'Oh my, I never thought of that either,' said the manager. Nor did I. It was Monday, but it was just like any Monday to me. Why they never thought of it, I don't know, perhaps because cops and hotel managers work weekends and confuse them with ordinary days. In any event I said, frostily, 'Well?'

The detective seemed somewhat peeved now, and he said, 'Look, this guy seems all right, I don't know what the fuss is about.' By now the manager had had enough, he had been watching me closely as the call was made and my composure evidently satisfied him. He was probably already thinking of the row my company was going to raise when I reported the treatment I'd received at his hands. He suddenly began pouring out apologies and explaining over again how they'd been bitten before by bad cheques, and he hoped I wouldn't hold anything against the hotel. I was careful not to show my relief, in fact I was more cool and disdainful than ever. When he stated he would be happy now to accept my cheque I didn't let it go at that, I said I was in need of a few dollars cash—'so I don't have to risk arrest everywhere I go'—and informed him I wished to write a cheque for $250. 'Of course, of course,' he said. So I not only got my bill paid but I made seventy dollars cash off the deal."

He Donates His Luggage

"Once, and this was when events weren't proceeding as smoothly as they might have—I'd hocked my good luggage, and my clothes though neat were on the seedy side—I tried the manager of a small hotel with a cheque and he too said nothing doing. No amount of persuasion would move him. Finally I said, 'My good man, rather than be angry, I must admit I understand your concern, because there are any amount of crooks and con-men on the loose these days. The laws are too lax. I'll go this minute to my bank and get a certified cheque. Or would you prefer cash?' So I left my luggage with him, walked out and never came back. My suitcase was an imitation leather thing I'd picked up at the Sally Ann for fifty cents and the only thing in it was a big rock I'd found in a park and wrapped in newspapers. So for fifty cents I'd dined, slept and imbibed a quart of scotch a day for three days, which was a reasonable exchange, I thought."

A Trip to the Locksmith

"Another time I was at a hotel and I could tell by the way the manager was eyeing me that he was entertaining certain suspicions. I'd been there about a week and I was trying to think of a way to get out. I knew he wasn't going to take a cheque just because I asked him nicely, and it being an ordinary Tuesday there was no holiday in sight to save me this time. He had already hinted a few times that he wanted a payment on my bill. Now I could have simply walked out and not come back, but there was one hitch: I was stone broke and at this juncture in history I possessed two pieces of luggage, one a cheap worthless suitcase, and the other a very expensive alligator item left over from my prosperous days of not so long before. I was dying for a drink but I didn't have the nerve to put another bottle on my bill. That would have been the last straw. The obvious answer was to take that good suitcase with me. I knew I could get an easy thirty bucks for it—I'd bought it with my signature for a couple of hundred at a good luggage shop, and it was like new. But that was a problem, how was I to get my suitcase past the desk?

"There was nothing in either piece of luggage but rocks and newspapers, so what I did, I emptied the good one and removing my jacket and tie and rolling up my sleeves I took the elevator to the lobby with the alligator suitcase in hand. It was open, see, but I'd turned the lock so it wouldn't close, and holding it with both hands I went to the desk and said to the clerk, 'Where's the nearest locksmith? This damn thing seems to be broken.' And I gave a little demonstration of how it wouldn't close. I was very businesslike about it and he could see I wasn't dressed for leaving, I looked like I'd been working at my suitcase trying to fix it myself and finally bursting with impatience and frustration was rushing out to find a locksmith who could do the job right. He gave me directions and I thanked him and went out the door and never returned. I quickly merchandised the suitcase, went to the Sally Ann and picked up another one for a buck or two, along with a fairly presentable sports jacket and tie, and with the addition of a couple of bottles of wine was on my way."

§

I asked Dan how he had been finally caught, the time he was sentenced to two years in Kingston.

Because of a Woman

"Because of a woman," he said, "the downfall of many a man. I was shacked up with this thing in Toronto, I don't know where I picked her up but we had a small apartment and were living off some money I'd accumulated in my usual manner. Among the establishments I patronized were jewelry stores. I'd purchase something expensive, off my mythical bank account of course, like a watch or ring or necklace, and then wholesale it to a gentleman I knew who was in the selling business, the buying and selling business. I received only a fraction of the value of the goods but it was a living. Then I made the mistake of getting careless, of becoming overconfident, because I'd been operating for a few years now without being caught. This woman friend of mine, as it happened, had a birthday, and by coincidence I'd recently come into possession of a bit of jewelry which I was about to get rid of promptly as usual. We were at home then and we were drinking a couple of bottles of scotch, and I said out of the bigness of my heart, 'Well now, since it's your birthday I'll give you a birthday present.' So I produced a lovely pair of diamond earrings worth a few hundred bucks and I said, 'Here you are, my dear.' They were in a velvet-lined leather box with the imprint of the store inside the cover. She was much taken with the gift and I said I'd bought it just for her because, you know, she was not aware of the nature of my business. She thought I was an honest man with some money in the bank.

"Well, she gushed over the earrings and said things like, 'They must be very expensive,' and like a complete fool I casually mentioned the price because my ego couldn't resist making such a fine impression. She was greatly impressed that the earrings were worth so much, more impressed even than I thought when I told her. A few days later I came home to the apartment with a bag of liquor and was greeted by two cops. My woman friend was there too, crying. I was arrested on the spot. What she'd done, she'd gone down to the jewelry store with the earrings and tried to return them and get the money. By this time the owner of the store didn't have a particularly high opinion of the cheque I'd given him, so he kept her hanging around while he made a phone call. That's all it took. Two years in the pen because of a greedy woman."

When he was released he tried working at several jobs but the lure of the bottle was too strong and he was soon on the road. I mentioned that I had grown up in New Brunswick and he asked me what part I was from. I told him.

"I know that town. I spent a week in jail there."

I asked him what happened.

A Man of God

"Well, as usual I was looking for a handout, and I saw, you know, there's this enormous big church at the top of the hill, so I thought I would hit up the priest for a few bucks. The priest's house was pretty posh looking too, there were a couple of cars in the garage. I said to myself, 'They're prosperous here and shouldn't mind contributing something to the welfare of the needy,' namely me. I knocked on the door and a young priest answered, he would be an assistant to the parish priest I imagine, and I said, 'Excuse me, Father, but I'm passing through town and I wonder if you could help me out. I've been looking for work for months now and I hear there's something in Cape Breton but I'm having a hard time getting there. Being a devout servant of God as you are and a Catholic like myself, I'm sure you wouldn't see a poor man forced to sleep in a ditch at night and go hungry in the morning.'

"He looked at me impatiently and in a cold voice said, 'How much do you want?'

"'Well, Father,' I said, 'I think I could get by with five dollars though I've got a long road ahead.'

"'Five dollars!' he said. You'd think I asked him for one of his cars. 'Why you must be crazy. I certainly won't give you that.' He said he'd give me a quarter. Twenty-five cents. Well I didn't climb all the way up that hill for twenty-five cents so I began to tell him that if it was during the Depression his offer would be tolerable, but with inflation and rising costs a quarter was only slightly better than nothing. I started into a lecture about Christ, how he'd given everything he had to the poor and requested that other Christians do likewise, his disciples in particular, and I said the last place I'd been was the United Church minister in Campbellton and he'd given me ten dollars, which didn't happen to be true, he'd given me three, but it was better than a quarter. Anyway, this priest, who looked well-fed enough himself, got quite annoyed with me and after a bit of arguing said, 'I'm not listening to any more of this. You're nothing but a bum, trying to live off others. You'd better leave before I call the police.'

"'Nothing but a bum, am l,' I said. 'You stand there with you're big fucking stomach sticking out while half the kids in this town are going around starving and you call me a bum? I'd like to know who's the real parasite between the two of us.'

"His face turned red as a radish and he started sputtering and he told me to get going quick or he'd have me thrown in jail. I laughed at him and turned and walked away. Well, I wasn't that far down the street, walking along taking my time, when the cops drove up and stopped. The good father must have called them soon as I left. To compound matters I had a bottle of rubby tucked in my belt under my shirt. I got a week in the county jail and then according to the script was told to get out of town. Before getting on the highway I paid a call on the Anglican minister, a nice old guy, and he gave me five bucks and bought me a bus ticket to Moncton. Some you win and some you don't."

Reuben

"The laws in this country leave something to be desired. I'm normally a wine drinker, but on Sunday in some strange town where are you going to get a bottle of wine? The liquor stores are closed and if you find a bootlegger he'll charge you double. A man in my circumstances can't afford to pay overly inflated prices. But I need a drink all the same so what I generally do is go to a drugstore and buy a bottle of rubbing alcohol. It's not the smoothest drink in the world but you can get used to it and it serves the purpose. Some drugstores are all right, they know what you want the stuff for and they don't argue. But then you get these donkeys who think they know what's best for you, they want to protect you from yourself, while you're standing there shaking and ready to fall apart, and they won't sell it to you. So just to be safe I give them a story, it might be the only drugstore for miles. I walk in limping, for instance, I say I got a terrible pain in my leg, or I tell them I've got arthritis in my shoulder, or I've strained my back. I ask if they've got anything I can rub on the sore spot to ease the pain. Once I hobbled into a place and asked if they had anything for the pain in my leg; I said I heard there was a liniment that was good for a pulled muscle. I was going to grope around and come up with the name of a brand of rubby when the dumb jerk behind the counter says, 'I've got just the thing,' and he rummages around and brings out a bottle of something, I don't know what it was, olive oil or something, and I looked it over and I knew it was not something that I wanted to drink. Meanwhile I've already spotted the reuben on the shelf, and I says, 'Well, uh, I don't know if that would work—how about this stuff here?' and I reach up on the shelf and take down a bottle of rubby. He looks at me, throws the bottle in the bag, says 'sixty-five cents,' and I walk out, only it's kind of embarrassing, and in my hurry to leave I forget to limp. As I'm going out the door the guy calls after me, 'It's working already!'

"Another time I was in a town in Ontario where they've got a race track, just a small town, and it was Sunday and I had a vicious thirst on. I was walking down the street and since I'd noticed this track on the way in I stopped a kid and said, 'I see you have some horse racing here.' He says, 'Yeah, that's right.' And I says. 'I used to know a man around here, he's got a couple of horses up at the track, what's his name now... And I look like I'm thinking hard, and the kid says, 'Might be Jack Duncan, he owns quite a few,' and I says, 'That's right, kid, Jack Duncan's the name. Think I'll pay a call on him. Thanks.' So I continued down the street till I came to the drugstore and I go in and say to the man at the counter, 'Hello, I'm working for Jack Duncan now at the track and we got a few sore horses. I gotta pick up some liniment.' 'Oh yes, certainly,' the guy says, very eager to be of help, 'how much would you like?' Well, while I was there I thought I might as well make the most of it, so I says, 'You better make it a gallon so I don't have to keep running down for it all the time.' I knew they sold it by the gallon in some stores, though I think they rarely sold it in that quantity for drinking purposes. It happened that this place had the gallon bottles, most likely because of the track with all those horses. I gave the man the money and he gave me a receipt and I walked out with enough reuben to keep the fires burning for a little while to come. Actually it was too much to carry around, but I chanced upon a few more bums and between us we got to the bottom of the bottle."

The Sally Ann

Things don't always run smooth, I try my best but I don't manage to get a hotel room every night. To keep up my usual standard of living requires a better than average income—maybe double the average— and it takes a good deal of effort to raise it. A bum's life is not all pleasure. I used to stay at the Sally Ann sometimes but not anymore. To my mind they're hypocrites, the Salvation Army. They figure themselves very holy bastards helping poor sinners and they feel quite proud of themselves. That's their kick, they force poor bums and winos to repeat prayers and sing hymns and carry on like trained monkeys in return for a sandwich and a bowl of soup, and it makes them feel full of virtue. The guys they throw handouts to are never let forget what common tramps they are and the scum of the earth who should be humble and grateful that a better class of person is stooping to help them. I remember once we were sitting at this prayer meeting we had to put up with, and there were special guests there, politicians or some rich contributors to the fund, and this Major was on the stage doing his best to impress them. He was there talking to these slummers and he was all smiles telling them what great work he was doing and how happy the poor down-and-outers were now they were being helped. And he says, 'And now we'll have a hymn.' And he turns from his guests and you know, the change in his face when his eyes moved from them to us—his expression suddenly went from mild and angelic to stern and commanding, and he says, 'We will now sing Onward Christian Soldiers' or whatever, and the way he said it and that dirty look on his face, it was like he said, 'All right you peasants, you will sing this hymn *or you don't eat.*'"

§

When he related this, Dan mimicked the man. He possessed an excellent mimic talent and he varied the voices for the different characters in his stories. Though we were sitting at that time in the sun in the yard, from the expressions on Dan's face you saw a Major standing in his stiff uniform on a platform at the Sally Arm, the smiling and ingratiating Major at one moment, then the ramrod parade square officer commanding his subordinates the next. "These days if I go to the Sally Ann I either get a voucher for a hotel room or I don't take anything," said Dan. "You don't catch me sleeping in their lousy dormitories. I'd rather sleep in a zoo."

A Man Who Saw The Light

"There are many crazy individuals in the world, people who get the feeling they're messiahs, they figure it's their duty to rescue lost souls, like they got a message direct from God himself. There was this one guy in Winnipeg who all of a sudden saw the light. He was a businessman and had a bit of money and he got it into his head he was going to help out the deadbeats around town. He'd have a prayer meeting once a week and when it was over he'd pass out money for food. I think it was two bucks for each bum. Naturally it was a popular gathering, a whole gang of us would show up and get our two bucks and go out and buy some bingo. Only the guy soon caught on where his money was going, and one day he announced: 'Gentlemen, I'm sorry to say that I'm disappointed in you. I've been given to understand that you're taking the money I give you for food and wasting it on liquor. I'm afraid this can't go on. From now on I will make an arrangement for you to eat at a restaurant and I will have the bill sent to me.' Well, I was sitting there with a few of my buddies of the time, and we'd all sat through that prayer meeting and it looked like we were going to be deprived of the wine we'd come for. When the guy finished his speech, which he'd delivered almost in tears, because he was indeed disappointed in us as he said, I stood up and in a solemn heartfelt voice said: 'Mr. Collins, what you have just said is the truth. It's a shame but it's the truth. There are men here who have been taking your money on false pretences and throwing it away on alcohol. It's disgraceful behaviour and unfortunately reflects badly on the rest of us who are trying our best to get back on our feet and resume living decent productive lives. We are not all drunkards and it would be an injustice to those of us who are sincere if we are included amongst those who have deceived you. I know you feel that your trust in us has been betrayed, but let me assure you that this is not entirely so. Some have betrayed you, but there are others who have accepted with gratitude your generosity and walked with heads held high into a restaurant and purchased much needed food. It was with a sense of dignity that we ordered and paid for our meal, and for this we are indebted to you. Now, Mr. Collins, I have a proposal which I hope you'll agree to. I've been down on my luck for some time around this city and I know most of the men in this room. I know which of them are responsible people and which of them, sadly, are slaves to drink. If you will give me the money you meant to distribute I will pass it around to those who won't waste it—and as for the others, for their own good, you can arrange for them to be fed at a restaurant as you planned.'

"Well, he was moved by my speech and told me I was an honest man and an example to the others. 'I can rely on you to see this is properly distributed,' he said, giving me a handful of bills. I spread the money amongst my buddies and we left and promptly got hammered."

The Travelling Salesman

"Some of these travelling salesmen are hard to take, they pick you up for company and they want to be entertained, see. I don't mind that because that's part of my business, I give them a few stories and a few laughs and then hit them up for a few dollars. But some of those guys are ignorant sonsabitches, you know the type, loud and arrogant and stupid. I remember this one fellow, I was making my way east and I was out around Brandon, and he gave me a lift. I was just in the car when he said, 'You're on the bum, eh?' And for quite a few miles I got a gratuitous lecture about bums on welfare who could be working, and how he himself had worked his way along and look where he was now, and he always believed in helping a man when he was down but he'd only go so far, the man had to help himself, he couldn't live off society without making his contribution. So I had to sit there while he gave me this line of bullshit, you know, he was very hearty about it, and he'd say things like, 'Now talking man to man' or 'Let's face it, pal', horseshit salesman talk, 'I may not have a college education but I've been through the school of hard knocks.' I just said yes, yes, you're right, a lot of people should be working who aren't, they're just too lazy. Myself, I said, I suffered shell shock in the war and have a small pension, hardly enough to live off. My nerves are very bad, but I travel around trying to pick up some work where I can. But it's not easy, I'm only able to work for a while, I said, never for a long stretch of weeks because of my condition. He reluctantly agreed that I was probably an exception, but continued flapping his mouth about bums and deadbeats. He was getting some sort of twisted pleasure out of saying all this to my face, you could tell he was proud as hell of himself. I don't think he paid much attention to my war story at all, he was still in his mind telling a tramp what he thought of tramps. Anyway we drove on for quite a ways and I was getting a bit hungry, and he says finally, 'Why don't we stop in at a diner along the way—don't worry, it's on me.' I couldn't stand the sonuvabitch but I was in the mood for a bite to eat, so I says okay, it's fine with me. We pull up at a roadside diner and he takes me in, and there are people in there sitting at tables, a quiet little place, and soon as we're in the door, he's got one hand on my shoulder, he says in this booming voice, 'Give this poor man a cup of coffee!' Now how about that? 'Give this poor man a cup of coffee.' Everybody was looking at us. So I says in my own booming patronizing horseshit voice, 'One moment, waiter, I didn't order any coffee.' Then throwing my last dime on a table I said, 'See this poor bastard gets a bromo-seltzer.' Then I turned and walked out leaving him with his mouth hanging open."

His War Record

"Speaking of a war pension, which of course I don't have—the closest I've been to a war was when I was living with my wife—one of my routines is to visit various Legions along the way and tell them my war stories and how hard times have got for me now. If I find the right mark I usually do all right. Clothes, food, hotel, money. These guys can get very sentimental about old soldiers down on their luck, I mean as long as you're not a babbling idiot. You have to be able to say the right things and play the right strings."

A Fistful of Socks

"You know, when you're a man like myself and you have a strong urge to take a drink you can find yourself doing some shameful things. I try to be a decent person but occasionally I fall short and sometimes it can be embarrassing. I recall once, it was in Edmonton, I was strolling around the streets and I walked into a small clothing store. I gave the owner a hardluck story, about how I had a job starting Monday but this was Friday and I had no money for a place to stay till then, and I wondered if he could help me out, give me a small loan which I'd repay out of my first pay cheque. Any amount would do, I said. I was asking him out of impulse and desperation, I had never borrowed money before, and so on. Now I was as usual clean-shaven, my hair trimmed and combed, my clothes weren't in tatters or anything, as you'd expect in the case of a wino. I'm very careful about that. As for giving out a good line I might say I am as proficient at this as any bum in the country. So this man, he was not too old, maybe thirty-five, he looks at me a minute, sizing me up, then says, 'I don't normally do this, but—' and at that point a customer came in. Excuse me, he said, he'd get back to me after waiting on the customer. I said okay, I didn't mind waiting at all. I knew I had him, he was plainly going to give me a donation. Well, he was at the back of the store showing the customer some shirts and I was waiting there, and the next thing I knew I'd picked up a handful of socks and shoved them under my jacket. Why I did it I'll never know. It's not like me to pull a trick like that. But before I could stop myself it was done. In a minute the fellow came back and handed me a ten dollar bill. 'I wouldn't give you this if I didn't think you were sincere, you impress me as an honest man and not just a panhandler. I've had tough times in the past myself, I know what it means to get a helping hand when you really need it. I hope this will assist you.' I felt a bit bad as I walked out of the store because he had been so generous to me. But I couldn't very well take the socks out of my jacket and put them back. I wasn't long out of the store and on my way to the nearest liquor store when, as fate would have it, a cop grabbed hold of me. He said, 'Where do you think you're going? I've been watching you. We don't want no bums on the street here. What's that you got under your jacket?' He was a right mean bastard. He pulled the socks out and said, 'I saw you coming out of that store, I thought you were up to something.' He had a hold of me by the arm so I wouldn't run away, and it was probably a good idea on his part because if ever I wanted to take my chances and run that was it. 'Take your hands off me,' I said indignantly. 'The gentleman in that store was so kind as to give me these socks.' The cop laughed in my face. 'Yeah, he gave them to you,' he said. He practically lifted me off the pavement dragging me back to the store. 'I found this bum with a bunch of socks on him,' he said to the owner. 'He says you gave them to him.' The cop had a self-satisfied sneer on his face. The owner of the store looked at me and it was a sad look indeed. It wasn't an angry look, it was a look of bitter disappointment and disillusionment. As for myself I could have easily crawled under the carpet if the cop had let me loose. Never have I felt so low. 'That's right, I gave him the socks,' the owner said. 'You can let him go.' The cop stood there amazed and speechless. Finally it occurred to him to unclamp his hand from my arm. I was as dumbfounded as the cop. I'll be damned if I could think of anything to say, and that is unusual with me, so I just slunk out of the store, ten dollar bill in my pocket and six pairs of socks in my hand. I sold the socks to some guy on the street for the price of a wine. This happened five years ago but I'll never forget the disappointed look on that store owner's face. I keep thinking that one day I'll return to his store and repay him his ten bucks and throw in another ten for the socks. The only obstacle is I'm not sure I'll ever have twenty dollars to spare and be in Edmonton at the same time. But it's something to think about. That man was a real Christian, if ever there was one."

Vegreville

"Most of the time I travel alone, I prefer it that way because otherwise you have to earn too much in the run of a day to pay expenses, but now and again I'll bump into one of my old partners and we'll be on the road together for a while. I remember once I was with my buddy Soft Coal and we were going through Alberta. Soft Coal is his nickname, his real name's Jim. I gave him the name because he once told a farmer we did a bit of work for, Jim was smoking some godawful tobacco and the farmer asked what in hell he had in that pipe, dried cowshit? Jim says, 'Nope, soft coal.' Anyway we were on the road and hadn't had a drive for a long time, so we were walking along and we came to this little town. As we were strolling into it Soft Coal stopped a young fellow and said, 'Hey kid, where are we, what place is this anyway?' The young fellow says, 'Vegreville.'

"Soft Coal looks at me then back at the kid. 'Beggarville, eh?' he says. 'Well there's two more beggars in 'er now.'

Tools of the Trade

As I was saying, appearance is most important in my line of work. You have to give the impression you're only temporarily on the skids. If you look too far gone the most you're going to pick up are dimes and quarters. You need to maintain a certain air of fallen respectability and look like you're worth saving. A bum who looks like a bum arouses loathing, people draw away from him like he's a leper. But if you look neat and clean and appear to be trying your best to manage through difficult times, and if you can interest your victim with a good story, then you can come to expect a five or ten buck handout. Now I'm a Christian Scientist, I'm well read and I've been in many discussions with priests and ministers who are naturally curious about my beliefs and interested in discussing theology. Mind you I don't get disputatious, I don't argue, I discuss. And when they see what an intelligent man I am they feel bound to help me get back on my feet. I always travel light these days, I rarely carry luggage or a pack. It's just too much bother. Occasionally I'll lug a small flight bag along, but I'm in the habit of losing these while drunk. Even if I've got only the clothes on my back I always keep on me a razor, a comb, a needle and thread and some shoe polish. Once I was putting the arm on an old guy with whiskers, he might've been a rabbi, this was in Ottawa, and he was digging out some change—this was another of my lapses, I normally don't stop people on the street, it's an undignified method of cadging and it's not productive. You suffer a lot of discourtesy for small returns. Moreover there's the danger of being collared by the law. But I espied this old character across the street and it flashed through my mind that he was a rabbi, and a man of the cloth is my natural prey. I hotfooted it across the street and gave him a quick story, and without saying anything he was in the process of crossing my palm when the arm of the law once again descended on my shoulder. And once again I had a bottle of rubby tucked in my belt. The cop gave me a frisking and turned up my possessions, the razor and shoe polish and the rest. He pulled me in and when I came before the judge the cop was there and in a voice quivering with righteousness and incredulity, he said: 'You Honour, this man is a *professional bum*!' It was like a revelation to him. The description, I might say, was quite accurate. I remember another judge I appeared before. I had been nabbed in the street this time also. As I stood in the court the judge announced in a most solemn voice that I was being charged with, if you can believe it, 'soliciting alms.' That was a new one for me. I felt like saying, 'Allah be praised, your Honour!'"

§

Well, Dan's stories went on and on, and I've only given a sampler. I told him he should write down the story of his life. He might have a best seller.

The Literary Life

"Oh, I've thought about being a writer and in fact I did write a book once. It was about my travels, all the places I've been. There's not a man in this country knows Canada as well as myself. I've been over every inch of it and more than once. I've been in just about every jail too. I wrote this book, or most of it, while I was in Toronto. I'd done some work house-painting, it was one of the times when I decided to quit travelling and get off the bottle for a change. Sometimes you get the feeling when you're on the road that it's all very futile and you'd like to stop and just get yourself together for a while. Also you can absorb your fill of hoosier cops and filthy little county jails. I joined Alcoholics Anonymous and got a member to sponsor me and he found me a job and a nice bachelor apartment and I saved my money. In the evenings I went to meetings and worked on my book. AA's not like the Salvation Army, they're fine people, salt of the earth, none of that holier-than-thou attitude; I never say anything against them. But this period didn't last, as you may have gathered, and I was back again on the bottle and the road. I took the book with me and kept working on it when I had a free moment. I'd do a bit of writing when I got a hotel room, lying on the bed with a quart of wine and a pencil and paper. Or I'd stop on the roadside and sit in the shade and scribble down a few things that happened during the day or the past few days or something I remembered. After a while I felt I'd more or less finished the book and just kept it in a flight bag and carried it around with me. I didn't know how to go about getting it published but I thought that when I got back Toronto way I'd look up a good friend there who writes for the Globe & Mail and have him see about it. In the meantime I was in B.C. and I had an itch to go up to the Yukon. I'd never been there though I've been up again a few times since. I'm a great admirer of Robert Service and I was curious to see the country he'd lived in. Well, my book was in the flight bag along with some old clothes I'd picked up and it was a couple of months since I'd finished it and I more or less forgot about it. I was sitting on the side of the road outside Whitehorse sucking on a bottle of wine and this old squaw came hobbling along looking like she hadn't had a meal in weeks. She asked me for a few cents so she could buy a bite to eat. I felt sorry for her but unfortunately I was broke. I'd scrounged enough for the bottle but not a cent more. So I says, without thinking, 'Here, take this bag, you might be able to sell it. There's some old clothes in there which somebody might buy off you as well.' She thanked me and went tottering off and I resumed my idle drinking. I didn't think twice about giving the bag away, it was only a burden to be carrying around anyway. If I wanted another one I could always find one easily enough. So I was sitting there with nothing much on my mind when it suddenly struck me what I had done. I'd given my book away. I jumped up and took off after the squaw but I never found her. She'd gone into Whitehorse and vanished. And that was the end of my literary masterpiece. You might wonder how I could do such a stupid trick. I wonder too. I would have to blame it on the drink which apparently took some alertness out of my mind."

The End Of The Sentence

I was in the middle of listening to one of Dan's stories when I was informed I had a visitor. The guard called my name about ten times before I realized it was me he was calling. The guards were always shouting out for one person or another, and not expecting to be paged myself I got used to ignoring them. It was "L'Anglais" that was wanted, someone said, and someone else came over and said to me, "You 'ave a visitor." A visitor? Me? How could that be, I wondered. Nobody even knew I was here.

I was shown into a narrow room with a long table divided down the centre by a screen. There was a bench at the table. On the other side of the screen was Bernard. He was smiling secretly. I sat down opposite him and said, "Hi."

"Hi." Then he started laughing quietly. "How's everything?"

"Good. How'd you know I was here?"

"I heard it on the radio. A Montreal poet." He chuckled to himself some more. "That was something. I didn't know you'd do it. It's a good sign. I've been thinking about it quite a bit, and I think it's a good sign. It's too bad you got caught."

"Yeah, well, it's not so bad. It's material for my memoirs. I've met a very interesting man here, listening to him helps pass the time away. In fact by sitting here now I guarantee you I'm missing a good story, because that's what he's doing down there, telling one of his stories."

"I won't stay long. Do you want me to go now?"

"Oh no. I didn't mean that. How long do they give you to visit?"

"Half an hour."

"Aren't you kind of, how shall I say it, crazy, I mean coming here? It strikes me as a foolhardy thing to do."

"Oh?"

"It's a wonder you're not on this side of the screen with me right now."

He continued smiling. 'I knew you hadn't told them about me. If you had they'd have been around to pay me a call before the radio broadcast. My first impulse was to change addresses immediately, but I thought: 'It's unlikely they'll torture him for information. And if he hasn't said anything by now I doubt if he'll change his mind and volunteer my name and address.' So I stayed where I was. I am, I have to tell you, impressed by what you did." He paused, then said, "You don't suppose this room is bugged, do you?"

"I doubt it. That would be a rotten thing to do. I don't think they care about anything here, it's just a place to keep men off the streets for a while."

"That's what I thought."

"What did you have to tell them to get in for a visit? Did they ask a lot of questions?"

"No. I just gave them another name, and I'd brought along a few papers of my own creation with that name on it, just in case. It was easy. I said I was a friend and they said go ahead. They were quite friendly."

Bernard's moustache was growing well, it was long and bushy.

"I brought you a book," he said.

"Yeah? What is it?"

He slid it through a slot at the base of the screen. It was an anthology of poems.

"Poems," I said. I felt like sliding it right back.

"You like poetry, don't you?"

"Sure. But... I don't get much of a chance to read in here. And I've already got a couple of books from the library."

"Oh. I thought you might like a book. I didn't know you had a library."

"Well, thanks, it was good of you. I appreciate it. I'll read it in my cell."

A book of poems in a prison. It made me shudder. What if the other inmates saw it? They'd have me then, I'd be unmasked for sure. A skin book, a comic book, a detective novel even. But poetry!

Nevertheless I kept the book, because it was thoughtful of Bernard to bring it. And he told me he had signed it in and couldn't take it back. Or it would be difficult to, rather strange to explain, and he didn't want to get involved in any situation that attracted attention. So I shoved the book under my shirt and hoped nobody would notice it.

"When do you get out?" Bernard said. I told him it would be a little earlier than expected, or was supposed to be—I wouldn't believe in my release until my feet hit the sidewalk. But from what I heard you got a day off for every week there.

"Give me a call," he said.

"You think I should see you? I think I'll just hightail it back to Montreal."

"That's what I was going to suggest. You never know. They might have connected you with me, or with someone. There are others around who are sweetening up cars. They'd have to think about that. They might watch you. That's why I said to phone. You could use a pay phone."

"Okay," I said. Bernard left and I was taken back to the common rooms. The next day my name was called again. This time I caught it.

"Someone wants to see you," I was told by the guard. Another visitor? I asked who and he said he didn't know.

I was escorted to an office. Sitting behind a desk was a sergeant. With him in the room were two young men.

"Have a seat," I was told. My two visitors didn't speak English and so the sergeant acted as a go-between and where necessary a direct translator. One of these gentlemen, I was informed, was the owner of one of the cars that I had operated on. His engine was ruined, he claimed. He was prepared to sue me unless I could settle with him now. His insurance didn't cover sugar in his gas tank. To save us trouble he would prefer to settle the matter out of court. He wanted fifteen hundred dollars.

"Fifteen hundred dollars!" I said. "Tell him he must be nuts. I've never had fifteen hundred dollars in my life or anything near it."

"You don't have a job?" said the sergeant.

"No. "

"How do you live?"

"I do a little freelance journalism." This was true, I had an editor friend at one of the numerous sex-and-gore tabloids in Montreal and wrote the occasional piece for them. With that and odd jobs like tutoring and delivering handbills and such I made enough to scrape by on. Mostly I never had much money. I'm an artist, not a capitalist.

The sergeant talked to the guy in French a while. The car owner was very animated. He kept giving me peculiar looks while he talked. His friend was impassive.

"He says you'll have to pay him," said the sergeant, "or he'll take you to court."

"Tell him to go ahead. I can't give him what I don't have."

There was more French conversation. Again I was told I'd have to pay. Only this time the bill was lowered to an even thousand. But it was all the same to me. I repeated that I had no money and I was unemployed. I said to tell the guy I was sorry I inconvenienced him, that it was nothing personal. When that was translated to him he started ranting. I didn't know what he was saying but it wasn't hard to imagine: "Nothing personal! What do I care about personal! My car is ruined and it cost me a lot of money. Does he know how hard it was to get that car, how I had to work and save and meet payments? Does he realize how I need it, I need a car to get to work, and how am I supposed to take my girlfriend out? Is he crazy or something, he doesn't even know me. Why did he pick my car? He should be locked up in a lunatic asylum. I want my money! Tell him he has to give me the money! Etc."

The sergeant finally concluded we were getting nowhere and said, "He's definitely going to take you to court and you'll have the burden of that debt on you for a long time, because he says he'll sue you for five thousand. And then you'll have to pay the court costs as well. Couldn't you borrow the money?"

"Not a chance. My friends are all poor too. So is my family."

"Well, why not get a steady job and pay him in instalments. Surely you could get a job, you're young and you've got an education."

'I don't have time for a job. I'm a poet. That's my job."

"Well, there's nothing I can do. You can expect to receive a court summons. Where will you be?"

"I don't know. In Montreal."

I was taken downstairs again, leaving a very angry ex-car owner. It was the last I ever heard of him. He obviously recognized a hopeless cause when he saw one.

I had two more visits of the same nature shortly after. I thought they were all asking too much money, though I shouldn't have been surprised;

humans are a greedy lot. One of my visitors was a woman. She was fat and did a lot of gesticulating and swearing at me. The other appeared to be a business-man. He spoke to me in English trying to make me realize the seriousness of my crime, and how it was my moral and legal obligation to reimburse him for the damage I'd done him. I didn't say much, but I said this much: "I didn't damage you. It was your car I damaged." That had no favourable effect. His car was part of him.

§

In the morning and evening when it was wash-up time I observed I was the only man there who brushed his teeth. The reason for this was simple: I was the only man who had a toothbrush. I didn't bring it with me, because like many of the inmates my happening to be in jail was a matter of pure circumstance; I had not planned it and so didn't bring with me the things I might need.

My second day at the prison I was taken to the infirmary for a checkup. The doctor was a portly and pleasant man, and I informed him that I had no toothbrush and I was in the habit of brushing my teeth before going to bed and when getting up. He pondered a minute, then went digging into a cupboard and handed me a new toothbrush. "I can give you this. But don't tell the others, it's not a standard practice to give out toothbrushes." I promised not to.

Did any of my fellow inmates ever wonder if I'd set out to commit my crime with a toothbrush in my pocket just in case?

§

On the one Sunday I was in the prison I went to mass. I wasn't impelled by a sudden regeneration of my lapsed Catholic faith. It was a combination of curiosity, to see what a mass behind bars was like, and of following the crowd. There was full attendance. It was one of the few breaks in the monotony of the week. It's possible an hour of Devil worship would have drawn the same crowd.

It was more or less an ordinary mass. As is said, when you've seen one you've seen them all. Except the sermon was in French. And the congregation was singular, being a hundred per cent males wearing drabby gray uniforms. About ten of them went to communion. I found that surprising, it surfaced an old prejudice which said men in prison had turned their backs on religion, scorning it as a refuge for women and poets and suchlike. But nobody snickered at the men taking communion. It was no problem, just a routine affair, apparently not seen as a sign of weakness or effeminacy. Well, that's good, I thought. I tried to pick out a few words of the priest's sermon but was not successful. I asked one of the French guys—there were a number of them who'd gathered around to listen to Dan's tales—I asked one of them later what the priest had said.

116

"Da same ol' ting, you know dat stuff, about da grace of God an' say your prayer an' da greatness of da Church. Repent your sin an' error of da pas' an' promise not to make dose same mistake again. Give your prayer an' your soul an' some of your money to da Church, eh? an' God is gone 'elp you, tabernac! An' den he talk about drinking, 'cause you know, mos' da guy in da chapel, dey're drunks an' dey're always in 'ere. Like me—dis is da secon' time I'm spending six month in dis 'ole."

§

The pencil strokes on my cell wall added up.

"You're getting out today," one of the French guys said to me.

"Yeah? You sure?" I was about ready to go too. Despite the diversion of Dan's storytelling the routine of the place was extremely boring and the confinement an affront to my free spirit. It was not really a very pleasant spot to be. Those barred windows, the high walls, the public toilets, the stubbly faces, the stale smells, the smoke in the air, the raw throats, the coughing and spitting, the cursing and swearing, the glazed eyes, the heavy boots on the cement, the shouting and hollering in the night, the lonesome foghorns on the river, the parading in lines, the locking of iron doors, the derelicts, the dead-end youngsters, the shuffling zombies. You can have it.

Around mid-morning I heard my name called by the guard. He was right, this must be it, I thought.

But it wasn't, not quite. "You go to the barber," I was told. I didn't want to go to a barber, my hair and beard were doing okay. "Do I have to?" I said.

The barber spoke good English and asked me how I wanted my hair cut. It was a regular barbershop inside the prison. "I hardly want it cut at all," I said. "Just this much." I showed him my finger and thumb with about a hundredth of an inch between. So he made a few clippety-clips with his scissors and pointed me at the mirror and asked if that was all right. I said it was. "You can shave yourself if you like," he said.

"I wouldn't mind giving my beard a slight trim," I said. "Can I borrow a pair of scissors?"

"No, we don't allow that," the barber said.

"Not even a little trim?"

There was a guard in the room with us and they exchanged glances. The guard shook his head.

"Sorry, we can't let you have scissors," the barber said.

"I won't attack anyone."

"Yes, I know, but it's the rule."

"Okay," I said. "Maybe I'll give my neck a shave. Where's the razor?"

There were a couple of sinks on the wall, and the barber pointed out the razor. It was a safety razor, very much a safety razor. It was attached to the wall by a chain and the blade was locked in.

When I was finished at the barber's I was escorted back to the common rooms.

"It won't be long now," said Dan. "Sorry you have to go, it was nice talking to you."

"Well, in a way I'm sorry to be leaving, but not very much. I enjoyed our conversations a lot myself. I wonder what time I'll be let out?"

I was impatient. Every second I expected the call to come for me. I wasn't absolutely sure I *was* getting out today either, because nothing officially had been told me. It would be a long evening if there was a mistake.

Dan was talking about becoming a university professor in the fall. He said he thought he could convince some university that he had a doctorate. He could forge the papers and then do some smart talking.

"What would you teach?" I said.

"Theology probably. Comparative religions. Being a professor sounds like a soft job. Running around the way I do I'm wasting my intellect."

At noon we went for dinner, and as I was leaving the dining hall a guard stopped me. "Come with me," he said. We went upstairs and I was told I was being released. They gave me my clothes and I took a shower and returned the gray uniform. An old geezer of a man was being released at the same time. He took his shower beside me, his body white and wrinkled. He didn't appear to be the least elated. Leaving to him must have become as routine as arriving. I watched him dress, his street clothes ragged and pathetic, the soles of his shoes coming off.

At the desk I was given my possessions back, and an account of the tobacco, papers and matches I'd bought, the money having been deducted from my small horde.

"Okay, you can leave by that door. And we don't want to see you back here again," said the sergeant.

"I'll accept that," I said.

§

I was welcomed by a flood of sunlight and an open street. The trees and grass were as green as could be, it was a clear and perfect day for walking out of jail. I stood for a moment to take it in, only a moment to take a breath of the summer air and soak up the feeling of freedom, and I was on my way.

After a few blocks of brisk walking I looked over my shoulder to see if I was being followed, remembering what Bernard had said. I stopped at a red light and though there was no traffic I stood and waited for the light to turn green, something I had never done in Montreal, and which is not done by anybody in Montreal or Quebec. But I didn't want to break the law. I mean I didn't want to get caught breaking the law and thrown back in jail. The way I felt, my peace of mind was in proportion to the distance I put between me and the Quebec Prison. I walked directly to the train station, going down the little streets on the hill, those fine old streets which I would not be able to stay around and enjoy. At the station I bought a ticket on the next train to Montreal, and with four hours to wait repaired to a nearby tavern. I thought of calling Bernard but decided against it. I didn't really feel like talking to him just then. It would be better to write him a letter. Or better still, never see or talk to him again. When all was said and done I was a poet, a thinker, an observer of life, not some bomb-throwing anarchist. Sober I never would have got myself into such a mess.

As I sat and drank my beer I reflected on that, on freedom, and what I'd better be prepared to give up if necessary to retain what share I had of it. It was far too precious an item to play fast and loose with. I had a good deal to think about, and while doing so ordered another couple of beers, and if I wasn't on my train when it pulled out it was because of some convivial English-speaking patrons at the next table. It's my guess they were the new-found friends who lugged me to the station and put me on a later train, for in the early morning I awoke and found myself back in Montreal.

ENDNOTE

This story took place some years ago and since then the Quebec Prison has ceased to function as a prison. It was subsequently renovated and for a time served during the summer months as a hostel for transient youth.

College Town Restaurant

The waitress was a stout country girl. You could tell she was from the country by the way she talked, for instance she would pronounce the word "now" like "nyow", or "house" like "hyouse". Her skin was coarse and she had an eyetooth in the front of her mouth, and there was a big mole on her cheek. And yet she was not entirely unattractive.

At some point, it would be around nine-thirty in the evening, a husky fellow came into the restaurant and sat at the counter. I gathered by the way he talked that he was from the country too, and he must have been from the same place as the waitress because he knew her. He carried a visored cap in his hand and placed it on the stool between himself and me.

"You're early tonight," the waitress said. She was washing cups behind the counter.

"I couldn't sleep. Harry brought his guitar over and they all got singin'."

"D'you want a coffee?"

"Yeah. Workin' hard tonight?"

"No."

He smiled broadly at her. She looked past him at the booths, to see if there were any unserved customers. The restaurant was packed but it would be a mistake to think a lot of money was being spent. The customers were mostly students from the highschool and the college and they put in hours over the same coffee or coke. Newbridge was a small town and the Castle Restaurant was about the only place you could go in the evening. There were more students standing around waiting to get a booth. Some of the stools at the counter were still unoccupied.

"How late d'you have to work tonight?"

"Twelve."

She got him his coffee and scribbled his bill out. She resumed washing cups.

"Yessir, they were makin' an awful racket home. I couldn't sleep to save me soul. I'll be glad when I get off this Jesus night duty."

The waitress said nothing, not looking at him. He sipped his coffee, staring all the time at her, smiling at her when he caught her eye.

"You're not sayin' much tonight."

"No."

"What's wrong?"

"Oh ... I'm mad at you."

Catching at this bit of banter the fellow said roundly, "Arh, now what did I do? I never did nothin'. What did I do?"

But she evidently lost interest before even starting.

"Nothing," she muttered, and went for a dish towel. In the meantime another waitress came behind the counter and filled four glasses with coke at the fountain. She placed them 0n the counter and wrote out the bill.

"How are *you* tonight, dear?" the fellow boomed, his red face looking eagerly at her.

"I'm fine."

"Are ya workin' hard?"

"Oh yes, I always work hard." She was a blonde girl of seventeen and talked as if she had adenoid trouble. The first waitress returned with her towel.

"We either work hard or we go," she said.

The blonde girl clutched the four glasses in her hands and left. The other waitress dried the cups and placed them on a tray. When they were all dried she set the trayfull on a shelf and stood facing the huge mirror behind the counter, touching her hair into place. l saw the face of the country fellow beside me beaming, and he smiled widely—his eyes were fixed on the girl, but her face in the mirror was passive and she seemed absorbed in her hair. A college boy sitting further down the counter shouted, "Quit looking at yourself in the mirror!"

The waitress flushed, and turned her head to him with a laugh. "What?"

"Don't be looking at yourself in the mirror."

"I was just seeing how bad I looked."

"Oh. That's all right then."

The waitress went down among the booths and came back with an order. The coffee was almost gone, and she put another pot on to percolate. Then she poured the last two cups from the old pot, put four lumps of sugar and a little bottle of cream on each saucer, and carried them to a booth. When she came back the big fellow leaned toward her and said,

"Unh—" like he was trying to start a sentence but didn't know what to put in it. She looked at him impatiently.

"What?"

He strained toward her a moment, and said, "Unh—"

She looked at him and went about her work. Then desperately he said, "That Lena's some crazy, eh?—"

He picked his cap up and slid onto the stool next to mine, closer to where she was bent over her dishes. "We had the guitar there—she got up to sing a song—" He stopped, hesitating.

The waitress said nothing, left her dishes, and without looking at him went to the other end of the counter to putter around. I felt the man still straining toward her, half off his seat, and leaning hugely over the counter. The restaurant was full and noisy with talk and the jukebox was playing. Nobody paid the least attention to anyone else. After a while the waitress came back and said to me, almost angrily, "I gave you your coffee, didn't I?"

"Yes, this was it here," I said, nodding at my empty cup. I was using the saucer for an ashtray. I revolved around on my stool and looked down at the booths for a few minutes. When my cigarette was down to a butt I stepped on it and paid my bill and went home.

The Newbridge Sighting

Flying saucers seem to be a common enough sight about the world, judging by what you read in the papers. The only person I know who ever saw I one was Alec Mooney. Alec was a bachelor of about fifty, a railroad man, a familiar figure in the Black Horse tavern and a conversationalist of some renown. The only thing wrong with his conversation was that he talked so fast he was almost unintelligible. But he was usually worth listening to until he got too many in him. Then it was impossible to understand a word he said.

Alec's job at the CN was shovelling snow in winter. He may have worked there in the summer, but I don't know. He said he did, He said he did very important work for the CNR, winter and summer. He drove the engines and handled the telegraph service, and he managed the station in Burnley from time to time. He was moreover a close friend of the big boss of the railroad, "Mr. CNR," as he called him. He delivered trains all over Canada for Mr. CNR and helped formulate policies for the railroad.

He regularly attended important meetings in Montreal where I believe he was an important member of the Board of Directors of the CNR.

Besides being a great railroad man, Alec was many other great things. He was a connoisseur of rum and drank about two or three quarts a day while on the job, driving the big engines, but the rum had hardly any effect on him.

"I know how to drink, drink, how to drink, I do, drink rum, I can, hear that, drink rum, don't feel a thing, I can."

He had to repeat himself when he talked because he talked so fast he had to come back and pick you up again so you wouldn't get lost too far behind.

He was, it must also be said, a great lover, and the girls he seduced while on his runs across Canada would make Casanova blush with shame by comparison.

Alec wore a finely trimmed moustache which gave him a distinctive, rather debonair appearance. He normally had on a railroad cap, but when he was dressed smartly he wore a black tam. He was tall with a rugged weather-beaten face, and looked like a sincere and honest man. You would have to believe him if he said he saw a flying saucer. I mean, if you had holes in your head you'd believe him.

But all the same, he was the first man in Newbridge who even claimed he saw a saucer. It was in the tavern that he made his announcement.

"You know them flying Saucer things, flying saucers, saucers, eh, you know them flying saucers, flying saucers?"

"What about them, Alec?" said Paul Ryan, looking over the top of his beer. "You been seeing flying saucers, Alec?" he said.

"Damn right, damn right, I saw one, I did, saw one last night I did."

"Aw, go on, Alec, you're full of shit."

"I did, I did, yes I did, the truth, Ryan, the truth by God, I saw one last, last night, I did."

Jimmy Skidd, who was sitting with us, said:

"Where'd you see it, Alec? Was there any little green men in it?"

"Didn't see any green men, I didn't, no green men, but I saw flying saucer you bet by God, yes, yes, I saw it, I saw it last night."

"Where'd you see it, Alec, now tell us that?"

"Out by the ball diamond, ball diamond, eh, yes, right there in the ball diamond, it came down, came down, it did, and landed right in the infield. How about that now, eh, flying saucer it was, couldn't have been anything else, anything else, nope, saucer, right in the infield."

"Alec, you're right out of your mind. Flying saucers. Did you go for a trip in it?"

"Don't be smart, don't be smart, Ryan. I know. I know. I saw the flying saucer, I did."

Alec stuck to his story, but that wasn't unusual because he always did, regardless of what he was saying. If he'd said he'd been on the moon that afternoon he wouldn't have denied it even if he'd been in that same chair all day.

"There must be marks on the ball diamond, Alec," said Skidd. "A big flying saucer couldn't land right there in the infield and not leave some tracks."

Alec paused a second and said, "Of course, tracks, there's marks, of course, marks on the ground, yes, it left marks, yes it did."

"Why didn't you tell the cops?"

"Maybe tracks gone now, you don't know. Can't tell cops, don't be crazy, what do cops know, mounties don't know nothing. They'd arrest me for telling lies, wouldn't believe me, believe me, you know the mounties, can't trust them. No, not saying anything, I'm not."

"Alec, you just made that story up," Ryan said. "You didn't see any flying saucer any more than I did."

But Alec was adamant. He cursed and swore at Ryan for not believing him, and said Ryan didn't know anything about anything.

"All right, Alec, why don't you tell the newspapers about your saucer? All kinds of crackpots are always telling the papers about seeing saucers, so you might as well get your two cents in."

"Going to, going to," said Alec, nodding his head swiftly and tossing down a drink of beer. "Yes, yes. Moncton Times, Times man called me up and wants story, wants to know all about it. Interview, he wants, he does, interview. Going to talk to man from the Times, I am."

"Well, that's great," said Skidd, "we should read about it in tomorrow's paper."

"Maybe, maybe, but you can't tell, can't tell. They might want to keep it secret, secret, government business you know, saucers, government business. Outer space, attack from outer space maybe, maybe, got to keep it quiet. Talk to man from the Times and we'll see, we will."

He nodded his head knowingly.

"Aw, that's all baloney," said Ryan.

"Go to hell, Ryan, go to hell, hell, hell with you, Ryan," said Alec.'

After all hands had quaffed a few more beers and Alec was still claiming he'd seen a flying saucer and that it had landed on the infield of the baseball diamond, Ryan suggested that we go look for the marks the saucer left.

"Don't be crazy," I said. "We're not going to walk all the way out to the ball park just to look for flying saucer tracks."

"Maybe Alec really saw a flying saucer," said Ryan. "How do we know? He's probably just the kind who sees them."

"Yeah, that's about the size of it."

"I don't know," said Ryan, tipping his glass. "If there weren't saucers flying around all these people wouldn't be reporting them every day."

"Well, you can go look for tracks if you like."

"Honestly now, Alec," said Ryan, "did you really see a saucer last night?"

130

Ryan was one of those inscrutable people that you never know is being serious or pulling somebody's leg. He never laughed, no matter what he or anybody else said, so you couldn't tell what was going on in his mind. But most of the time he wasn't serious about anything he said.

"What were you doing up by the ball park last night anyway?" he asked Alec.

"Looking it over, over, I was, looking the field over. Might coach ball team next season, asked me to, they did, asked me to coach the All-Stars. Got to check the field, that's what I was doing, eh, check the field, might coach team. Saw flying saucer, came down, whooosh, came down, it did, just out of nowhere, all bright and shining, whooosh, down on the field, almost scared me to death, I was."

"And then it just flew away?"

"Oh, about two minutes, two minutes it was on the field, two minutes, three minutes, and windows, windows in it, see, and all lit up, windows, and I saw queer-looking guy, strange, like a monster, peeping out the window—"

"You never said that before," said Skidd. "You mean you saw one of these outer space creatures?"

"Sure, I did, I did, yes, I did, saw him in the window, head there, head, coloured orange, orange sort of, see, orange, crazy-looking guy, man from Mars probably."

"There you go, now," said Ryan. "If Alec can describe things in that detail, then they must be true."

"Goddam right, damn right, Ryan."

131

"We might be in for an invasion," said Ryan.

"That's the truth, truth, that is, by God, see."

Then Ryan said that the only thing to be done was the newspapers must hear about this sighting. He ordered another round of beer and said we'd have to call the Moncton Times and give them the story.

" This could make Alec famous," he said. "The first UFO sighting in Norwich county."

"What about Alec's interview with the Times man?" said Skidd.

"We can't wait for that. We have to get Alec on the phone right now with the story. The interview might be too late. Someone else is liable to see the saucer and Alec would miss his chance."

By now Alec was on his eighth or ninth pint and Ryan was telling him to drink up. Alec's capacity was on the limited side, and he was clearly feeling the effects of what he'd drunk. He was grinning foolishly and nodding his head to everything Ryan said.

"We'll get you on the phone and you give the story to the Times," Ryan was saying. "You'll be a big man after this."

"Right, Ryan, right, Ryan, big man, I am."

There was a pay phone in the tavern just inside the entrance and we all got up and gathered around it.

"Just tell your story, nice and straightforward," said Ryan, dialing the number.

He dropped the money in for the call and got hold of the newsroom. "Hello, I have a story that might be of interest to you," he said. "A man here in Newbridge has seen a flying saucer... Yes, that's right, a flying saucer. His name is Alec Mooney, an employee of the CNR... It landed on the infield of the Newbridge ball park... That's right, no kidding, he got a firsthand look at it, Alec Mooney's his name... about 9:30 tonight... yes, he's here. He's very excited about it, he saw one of the creatures in the machine too... Yes, here he is... he's very nervous, he can hardly get control of himself, but I'll I put him on."

Alec was pushed onto the telephone and began to relate the details of his sighting. What he gave was a thorough enough description, only it's unlikely the guy at the other end got a single word out of it. But Alec went on a mile a minute until he had his story out, and then Ryan took the phone again.

"You get all that?" he said. "What did you say?... Yes, he speaks English... I know, he's just very shook-up about it all, almost in a state of shock, I'd say, but it's the real thing... Mr. Mooney is a well-known citizen of Newbridge, and if he says he saw a flying saucer you can be sure it's the truth... It was at the Newbridge ball park, around nine-thirty this evening... The ship he saw was round, about 60 feet in diameter, and it was glowing all over, and in a window he saw one of the passengers... that's right, he was orange-coloured and had some kind of ugly horns sticking out and one big eye in the middle of his forehead, and he—or it, or whatever it was—was bald as an egg... The saucer stayed about three minutes... Mr. Mooney was hiding behind the backstop, and then it took off, faster than the eye could follow... Traces? Oh yes, there are marks out on the field where it landed. This has been confirmed by Mr. Mooney, and an investigative team from the Air Force base is expected to look at them tomorrow... That about covers it... yes, that's about it... Yes, I believe there were other witnesses, but I don't have their names at the moment... Certainly, Mr. Mooney would be glad to see a reporter tomorrow. We expect he'll be seeing many reporters... I'm a friend of Mr. Mooney's, I've known him since we were kids, I'll be only too happy to vouch for anything he says—pardon me, it's getting very busy around here, you can hear the noise... I'm sorry, some officials have just arrived. You've got everything?... all right... in tomorrow's paper. Good... fine, goodbye... pardon me?... yes, fine now, I have to go... thank you very much, I hope you've got everything right... that's right... tomorrow. Goodbye."

Ryan hung up and said: "Time for another round."

The next day the story appeared on the bottom half of the front page. It was headlined: *UFO in Newbridge?* The story went on to say:

> *A mysterious flying object was reported to have landed in Newbridge last evening.*
>
> *Witnesses to the incident say the strange craft set down in the local ball park and remained there several minutes before suddenly taking off with blinding speed.*
>
> *Mr. Alec Mooney, an employee of the CN and one of those who made the sighting, described the object to this paper last night.*

In a state bordering on nervous shock, Mr. Mooney said: "I never believed in flying saucers before, so you can imagine the start it gave me.

"This thing was about sixty feet in diameter and shaped round, and part of it seemed to rotate when it was in motion.

"From where I stood I could see windows, like portholes, in the machine and looking out one of these windows was an unusual creature.

He was orange-coloured and his skin glowed, like there was a light inside him, and on his head there were two horn-like objects, possibly antennae.

"It was horrible."

Authorities are in the process of investigating the incident.

The sighting is the first reported in the Newbridge area and has all citizens out looking for the possible return of the ship.

The article caused a considerable stir in Newbridge, and by mid-afternoon half the town was up at the ball field to see where the saucer had landed.

The opinion of most of the citizens, as they made their way to the ball park, went something like this: "That crazy Mooney, he's made up stories about everything else, and now he's gone so far as to get himself into the papers with a story of flying saucers!" All the same they went to look.

And when they got to the park their skepticism changed to wonder, and then even to belief. Because out on the ball field protected by a cordon set up by the RCMP were, in fact, the marks left by the strange machine from outer space.

Three depressions in the earth, one between first base and second, one at shortstop, and one between third base and home plate.

"There might really have been one, you never know," they whispered. "How else can you explain those marks out there."

It was adjudged that the marks were made by tripod landing gear. Authorities from the RCAF Base near town duly arrived to check the markings, and Alec was immediately located for questioning.

"Very strange," said one of the Air Force officers.

"Could be a hoax, but what motive could he have for inventing all this? *Something* he saw seems to have addled his brain."

When interviewed Alec stuck to his story. He had seen the saucer, it had landed, he'd seen a man in it, and then it had taken off. Did it have tripod landing gear, he was asked.

"What's that, what, what, sure it landed, landed, I am."

It was explained to him what the landing gear was, and he said, "Don't know, how could I know, dark, dark it was, couldn't tell, had to have landing gear, gear, had to, had to land, eh, it came in, came in it did and landed on the infield, I saw it, I did."

Alec's picture appeared in the Times next day and he was instantly a famous man around the county, and the Air Force officers stopped questioning him because to begin with they could scarcely understand what he was saying. And he seemed to say all things at once, so they didn't know what to make of him.

Samples of the earth on the ball diamond were taken and sent to the Federal laboratories in Ottawa. All ball games on the field were suspended as though it was sacred ground, and the town council considered designating it an official tourist attraction. But after a few days the park was in use again, because there was nowhere else to play ball, and the schedule was getting held up. Tourists, if they liked, could still look at the place where the saucer landed, when there wasn't a game going on.

Some time later a report came back from Ottawa saying there was nothing whatever that could be deduced from the sand from the ball park. It was just ordinary sand, and there was no radioactivity or pieces of metal or anything. There was just nothing.

But that didn't prove there wasn't a space ship. It merely meant that if there was, it had left no traces aside from the indentations of its landing gear.

A few months after the sighting the same bunch of us were sitting around a table at the Black Horse. Alec was telling us that he'd just got back from Toronto where he'd been talking with Mr. CNR who was hinting about retiring soon.

"See, Mr. CNR, he says Alec, Alec, he says, got to retire, retire one of these days, see, he says, and I says yes, Mr. CNR, you're getting old, getting old, I said, I did, and he says, Alec, Alec, Alec, we need a new man, new man he says, to run railroad. New man, see. Yes, I says, yes, need a new man, I says. Alec, Alec, he says, how'd you like run the railroad, run railroad, he says, he did, said to me, Alec, how'd you like run the railroad, railroad, run the railroad, he said, and I says, well, don't know, don't know, eh, don't know says I, busy, busy these days, busy. Air Force after me, Air Force, I says, Air Force want me work on flying saucers, see, says I, flying saucers, know all about them, I do, maybe next year, Mr. CNR, maybe next year, take the job, maybe, I will."

"Do you do much travelling now that you're famous, Alec?" said Skidd.

"Oh yes, oh yes, never stop, not me, on the go all the time. Got a lot of business, business, I have."

"How are the women treating you?"

"Don't mention it, women, oh, yes, should've seen the blonde, blonde, blonde in Toronto, built like this, like this, see," and with a sly look he shaped out the measurements with his hands. "She said, blonde said, Alec, should be a movie star, she said, that's right, Alec, she said, should be in movies, well, I led her on, I did, led her on, led her on, looked like Marilyn Monroe, better, better though, Alec, she says, how'd you like come to my place for a drink of rum, rum, see, and..."

And Alec went on to describe his evening with the girl in Toronto. At length Ryan said:

"Seen any more flying saucers, Alec?"

"Nope, no more, not since last one, no, none lately. Showed you, eh, Ryan, didn't believe me, flying saucer, didn't believe me, eh? You saw, saw the tracks, place where tripod landed, eh?"

He laughed and poured down a good drink of his beer. "I know what I saw, I know, can't fool me," he said. "Yep, flew right in, it did, flying saucer, from Mars likely, landed in ball park. Didn't believe me, did you, Ryan? Showed you, ha, showed you, I did. Yes sir, space ship, landed right in Newbridge."

Of course what Ryan had done that night was gone up to the park with a shovel and made those three holes. But all he said was:

"By God, Alec, I'll never doubt your word again."

"Taught you, eh Ryan, showed you, I did, yes sir."

Spanish Jack

There were three English sailors, you see, and they were off a pulp boat down at the Station Wharf, this boat was finishing loading up and the sailors were on shore and they went to the Black Horse, which happens to be the only tavern in town. They were drinking beer and starting to feel pretty good and they were talking in that English kind of accent so you could hardly understand them. But nobody took offence because sailors were common enough around town during the summer, there was always a boat in loading pulp, they came from all over the world, Germany, Italy, Ireland, Norway, England, all with different colours of flags and all the sailors talking foreign languages. You could partly understand the English guys but you had to pay close attention and even then it was hard to get all the words no matter how close you listened.

Jack McIntyre, the old guy who owns the tugboat, was in the Black Horse too, you'd see him there every day, he'd come in about four in the afternoon and sometimes he'd go home for supper, and sometimes he'd stay right through till closing time at eleven-thirty and then go home. By that time he'd be pretty drunk. It was amazing how he could keep it up because he was more than seventy-five years old. Most of the time he had a stub of a cigar in his mouth, it might have been the same cigar all the time, because it was never lit and was always the same length, about two inches long. And he had stubbly whiskers, like two or three days growth of beard, and that seemed to stay the same too, which seems impossible, but I don't think I ever saw him clean shaven, or with his whiskers any longer. He'd been operating the tugboat for probably fifty years, it looked like the same boat, a worn-out old tub. It was called *Flora*, after his wife. They'd been married probably fifty years, she was about the same age as Jack. You didn't see her much. She stayed in the house most of the time, sometimes she'd come out to buy the groceries. She was scrawny and wrinkled like people get at her age. Some people say she used to be a very good-looking woman when she was young, and Jack was even supposed to have been quite a good-looking fellow too, but you couldn't tell it to look at either of them now. You often hear that about old people, how strong they once were, or how smart they were, or how much work they could do in a day, things like that.

Well, Jack was in the Black Horse, and he was sitting beside the English sailors who were drinking beer pretty hard and doing a lot of talking, everything "bloody this and bloody that", and after a while one of them turned to Jack and said, "Hey mate, where can you get a piece of tail in this bloody town?" or something like that, because they'd been talking about skin, like you hear a lot of in taverns, how much they'd got in different ports, and how rough it was being on a ship in the middle of the ocean and having to do without a woman. They were young guys.

"What's that?" said Jack, who didn't understand because of the accent.

"We're tryin' to get bloody laid," the guy repeated.

"Where can we find some nice birds," which was their word for girls.

When Jack finally understood them he said: "I don't know nothin' about that, not at my age, my skinnin' days is over," he said.

Well, the English guys laughed, and they bought Jack a beer, because they thought if they weren't going to get laid at least they could have some fun with this old guy.

"What d'you mean, you're too bloody old?" they said.

"There's guys ninety years old still doin' it five bloody times a night. I heard of one old bastard who knocked his wife up when he was a hundred."

"Well, I don't know about that," said Jack, "maybe it's true, I don't like to say it ain't to your face, but all I know is I'd just as soon sit back and drink my beer and then go home to bed. I'll leave the skinnin' around to the youngsters. My old woman's a bit past her prime too."

142

The sailors wouldn't let him off with that. They said if Jack got his hands on a young girl, some real fine looking stuff about eighteen he'd soon forget how old he was.

"Now that might be so," said Jack, "but where am I gonna find a girl of eighteen? The only whore in town is Ma Murphy and she's damn near as old as I am. And you wouldn't catch me goin' near her anyhow, I ain't lookin' to get the clap. If you boys want to give her a try I'll tell you where she lives."

"How bleedin' old is she?"

"Oh, she'd be... I guess she'd be around fifty-five, fifty-six. She's a little hard on the eyes too, I might warn ya."

"The hell with that," one of them said.

"She might be better than nothin'," said another one. "If you're drunk enough you don't know the difference."

Well, they talked on about what they would do, and they bought Jack more beer, so he hung around most of the evening, not bothering to go home for supper.

As Jack got feeling better he became more free and talkative on the subject of skin, and he related tales from the past, some of which might have been true and others of which probably weren't. And after a while he began saying things like, "I still got a bit of the tomcat left in me, despite me age. I ain't all I was but I ain't exactly washed up yet either."

And the sailors said why didn't he put the works to his wife when he went home? "She's probably bloody-well starvin' for a good piece of ass," they said.

"Well, I don't know, it's been quite a while and it might come as a shock to her. She's liable to drop dead from shock."

"It'd do the old bird good."

"Well, maybe so, but there's another thing. The wife's a fine enough woman and she was once something to look at but she's gettin' on and a woman loses some of her physical looks with age, if you see what I mean. I don't know if I could still get it up for her, good a woman as she is. Now if she was maybe twenty or thirty years younger I would rush home right this instant and make her happy."

The sailors looked at each other. They grinned. Finally one of them said, 'Old man, I got just the bloody thing for you, it'll make your old prick stand up like a bloody ramrod, and it'll make your wife look like a sixteen year old virgin."

"What would that be?" said Jack. A look of suspicion came into his eye.

"You ever hear about Spanish Fly?"

"You're damn right I did. But I don't believe it. And if I did I wouldn't touch the stuff. I heard stories, but I never seen it, and I never believed the stories because people are always making things up."

"But this is the real thing, this works just right."

"I don't know, now... Lemme see it."

"Well, it ain't exactly Spanish Fly, it's something better. We picked it up in Denmark. I'll put some in your beer."

"Hold on, hold on," said Jack, putting his hand over his beer glass. "Now I don't want to try none of that foreign stuff. I ain't sayin' it'll work, but if it does then it ain't for me. From what I heard you take that stuff and you go right crazy, runnin' after dogs and cats and anything in sight, climbin' onto fire hydrants, lampposts, anything, and you can't stop for days. Either way, I don't want it."

"You got it all wrong, old man. You been hearing wild stories from guys who don't bloody know what they're talking about. Anyway, this stuff is mild, all it does is get you up and you get real horny and you'll give your wife a nice time. And it only lasts about an hour, two at the most. We all tried it. We wouldn't give you something that's gonna cause you harm."

"I don't care. Thanks all the same, but I gotta watch me health at my age."

"Waiter, bring us another round," said one of the sailors.

About an hour and a half later Jack was saying, his voice a little thick, "Now you're sure this stuff works, you ain't tryna make a fool of me, I mean what's it like again?"

For the tenth time the sailors explained the joys and glories, the wildest sex pleasures that a man got when he took their love potion.

There's no doubt that Jack would never have taken this potion if he hadn't got drunk from all the free beer. He watched while they dumped the powder in his glass.

"Only a little," he said, "not too much."

"We'll just give you half a portion," they said, though they probably gave him at least a full one, and maybe a lot more.

"Well, here goes," said Jack, and he belted the glass of beer back. He sat there a moment, working his lips, concentrating, waiting for something to happen.

"Don't taste like nothin'," he said. "Can't feel nothin' yet either."

"It takes a while. It creeps up on ya, like."

They got him another beer and he took a drink, a sort of abstract look on his face while he tried to experience the effects of the powder.

"You guys must be tryna fool me, I don't feel nothin', it don't work."

"You wait. It'll fuckin' well work." And the sailors laughed. Jack laughed too. "Might be I'm too strong for it," he said, "maybe it's like drinking, I can handle me liquor, it don't affect me much at all."

When closing time came around, which was not long later, Jack said, "Well, thanks for the beer, me boys, and I don't know about that other stuff."

"You'll see when you get home."

"Could be I'm startin' to feel a bit horny now. I better get movin'." He stood up, weaved a bit, then said, "You know, I do feel a bit funny, come to think of it."

The three Limeys laughed, coughing on their beer.

"Watch out for stray dogs, old man, and don't rape no bloody fire hydrants."

Well, old Jack staggered out of the Black Horse and along Water street and down by the railroad station, which was the direction he took to get home. It was a fine summer night, mild and starry, and the station was by the river and the waves slopped up against the wharves. Jack followed the track along side the old log boom that wasn't used anymore. His house was about a quarter mile up the track and overlooking the river. He was drunker than normal because as long as the sailors were paying for the beer he had made a point of taking advantage of a good thing.

By Jesus, he was thinking, I can feel it sure enough, them Limeys was right. Oh boy. He had sort of an itchy tingling feeling at the end of his knob, an impatient kind of feeling that something better be done about it. It was still hanging there but he knew, he knew for certain that it would come around readily as soon as the right occasion arose, else why would it feel that way? An unfamiliar wave of fierce passion or something like it ran up and down his body. It was especially strong at the base of his spine, and in his bowels, but the real feeling was at the end of his tool, it was like it was itching inside. He pulled his zipper down and rubbed at it a bit, trying to cool it down. But it had no effect. Lord Jesus, he thought, what's goin' on'? Goddammit I'm horny, holy suffering' Christ! That stuff was powerful.

He quickened his steps, stumbling along in the dark, hurrying and staggering to get home. He could see the light left on in the kitchen ahead and he panted his way almost trotting now over the cinders beside the tracks. The waves washed in against the track embankment but he wasn't paying any attention to that.

"Flora for Jesus sake wake up if you're asleep 'cause I'm comin' to get ya!" he shouted as he burst in the door. Hopping around in the kitchen like there was ants in his drawers he tore off his clothes, getting caught in a pantleg and falling down on the floor, rolling around and struggling to get those clothes off.

"What's goin' on down there?" Flora appeared at the head of the stairs in her long flannel nightie. Her eyes popped wide open at the sight of her husband rolling around on the floor with half his clothes off.

"What in—have you gone crazy? What in the world are you doing?"

"I'm comin' to get ya! Holy liftin' Jesus I'm on fire—"

Flora stared at him. She looked like she was going to faint on the spot. One hand went to her open mouth. Her teeth were out for the night and her little mouth was all sucked in like an old person with no teeth, which is what she was.

"You—you're drunk—you've gone out of your mind—"

By now Jack had everything off but his shirt and socks, and kicking the rest of his clothes aside he staggered sideways a moment, regained his balance, braced himself, looked up the stairs at her, then took off at a run up the steps. Flora squeaked, turned and ran into the bedroom, trying to close the door behind her. But there wasn't time. Jack pushed the door open and the next thing he had her on the bed with her nightie thrown on the floor.

Flora was whimpering and squeaking and pushing at him because she'd just awakened and was not in the mood for a sexual encounter, besides being long out of practice. The sight of Jack standing in front of her had half petrified her. It was something she hadn't laid eyes an for a long time, his old member pointing upwards at her like a cucumber, bobbing up and down as he made his way unsteadily towards her. Then it all happened in a rush, his tearing and tugging at her nightgown and then it was off and she was thrown on the bed and suddenly he was all over her. He was panting and growling like an old bear.

"Stop it," she protested, but Jack didn't hear her, he was beyond containing himself, rummaging his face over her body, her wrinkled old skin, her tiny breasts like two deflated prophylactics, his big rough hand clenching a loose handful of her buttock. In his mind now, drunken and confused the way it was, she was Flora in her youth again, robust and pretty and full of vinegar.

He had one breast in his mouth, practically the whole thing, and then a strange sound, an awful moan and growl like you might hear somewhere deep in a jungle came out of his throat, and—though I hate to say it, but it's true—he bit. His teeth clamped together like a vice, they were his own teeth, strong and yellow and as good as they always were, they came together like a starved dog sinking its fangs into a hunk of meat.

Flora shrieked. Instantly Jack realized what he had done. He paused. His mouth was full with a wet and rubbery substance. With blood dripping over his lips he turned his head and spit out on the floor.

§

Five minutes later he was clumsily tying a bandage on the left side of Flora's bleeding chest. She was unconscious, her face gray and shrunken, tiny whimperings coming out of her.

When the bandage was on Jack went to the phone and called an ambulance. His penis was still itching and burning, even now, but he didn't feel too horny anymore, he felt sick and bewildered.

"The wife's had an accident," he said into the phone. "She... she, uh, she cut herself, I think, somethin' happened to her... I don't know for sure..."

Well, the ambulance came and they loaded Flora into it, and Jack stayed at home while they took her to the hospital. He wondered why the ambulance guys had stared at him so oddly. Then he went into the bathroom and noticed his face in the mirror and the blood on his stubbly chin whiskers.

Despite her age, Flora survived all right, they sewed up the place where her old breast had been, but she wasn't hesitant about telling the people at the hospital what had happened. As a result a couple of policemen came to Jack's place and took him off to jail.

He wouldn't say anything that night about what had happened. He was too embarrassed or ashamed or confused. He just wouldn't say a word. He went to sleep in his cell. The next day they got the story out of him.

"You know, I was thinking I dreamt it," he said. "I woke up and I remembered a terrible dream, a regular nightmare, and I thought my Jesus that's an awful thing to dream about, and then I noticed that I wasn't home but it looked like I was in jail. I thought first I'd got too drunk and that's what'd happened, they'd got me staggering around the streets or into some mischief. So to straighten myself out I began going over what I remembered of the night, and I remembered these sailors who bought me all the beer and then I realized Holy Christ I don't think that was a dream after all. Then I couldn't think too much more and I said to myself, I'll wait and see what they tell me, because it's probably okay, they'll just tell me it's okay and I'll figure out later what was a dream and what wasn't. But my worst fears are come true. And it ain't my fault either, it's those goddamn Limeys who give me the Spanish Fly, and now look what happened. You're sure Flora's all right? She ain't gonna be too happy with me after this."

Flora wasn't too happy it was true, and for a few days she insisted that her husband had to be put in an insane asylum because clearly he had gone round the bend. She was told Jack's story about the three sailors but she said at first, "That's only a lie he made up to try and get out of it. I never heard of such a thing." But after a while she changed her mind. As she said, "Maybe it's true, maybe it ain't, but maybe it is because he never done nothin' like that before. Anyway if they put him in prison or in the asylum what's gonna happen to me? I can't work at my age and I got the rheumatism and that old age pension won't keep me goin', not these days with prices what they are."

Whether what Jack had taken in his beer was really Spanish Fly or whatever it was, the police couldn't find out, because the pulp boat had sailed early in the morning while Jack was still sleeping it off in his cell.

A lot of people don't believe there is such a thing as Spanish Fly. They figure it's only something you hear about in dirty jokes or farfetched stories. The police, I don't know what they thought, they didn't know whether to believe old Jack or not, and it's possible they didn't, but because he'd been around town a long time and had never gotten into any trouble other than a bit of hard drinking, and because Flora didn't want charges laid they dropped the whole matter and let him go.

Flora was soon out of the hospital, her wound healing very well for an old lady like her, and they were living together again. Jack, to show his repentance, even stopped going to the tavern after work. At least he stopped for two days, but he couldn't take any more than that, and the third day he was sitting in the tavern as usual drinking his beer. But, as he assured Flora, he would not let sailors put anything in his beer again. When he relates his story to guys at the Black Horse, and he doesn't mind telling it— "...and I went home, I tell ya, and I was so be-Jesus horny I bit one of the wife's tits clean off, so help me God—" he warns the boys to watch out for them Limey sailors and for Christsake to keep away from the Spanish Fly because it's deadly as dynamite.

Many people now, the guys around town, they don't call him just Jack now, or old Jack, they call him Spanish Jack even though he's not a Spaniard.

A Cold Frosty Morning

James my old schoolmate with his moral
superiority the guy must practice before the mirror
looking angelic and fulfilled but like a fool I told him
okay I'll go put in a few hours at this place I'll paint
some damn walls why not I can be as virtuous as you
it'll give me all the moral complacency I need for a
month or two I'll be able to wake in the mornings and
I'll think of that good thing I did and feel like a
perfectly decent human being not some whatever I am
the guy who opens his eyes in the morning and there's
that moment that instant when it all seems like so
much horseshit thinking for Godsake is that the best
you can do with your life writing *poems* but then what
if Shakespeare said that and quit before he started and
the other great bards like myself so you push on
despite the doubts rejections and nobody cares

James of course bounds out of bed in the
morning to help the poor and falls asleep at night his
conscience glowing knowing he's been selfless again
it's perfect for his ego who he's helping he's helping

154

himself using these impoverished bastards the poor and dispossessed the worst of it is it seems to work though he might be putting it on and one day he'll jump off the Jacques Cartier bridge

When he asked I first said the hell with that look James I'm too busy working on my verses I don't have time for helping out pensioners yes yes I know I should but you're better at it than me and what can I do I'm no carpenter or house-painter I'd only make a mess of things tell the poor I appreciate their problems and I wish them well and if ever I get rich you can be sure I'll pass along a bit of money to do my bit well I mean what could I do he was trying to put me on the spot with his do-gooder pressure I told him look it's your business helping them that's your calling in life I can give you some poems of mine and you can read them to the old bastards everybody's got their own vocation as Father O'Donnell told us at Sacred Heart High you remember

It's okay I'm not trying to talk you into anything Geoff he says if you can't help it's all right I know you're busy and understand something like this would be difficult for you let's forget about it I only thought I'd mention it I'm looking around for some guys who can offer a little free time that's all I can't expect everyone to volunteer but if ever you've got a morning to spare let me know and I'll give you something to do there's always something some of these people the conditions they live in as you can imagine old crippled undernourished living in the worst dumps it's a shame

§

Difficult for me you see what I mean that superior attitude oh yes he understands it'd be too much for me I didn't have what it takes to get above myself and my selfish interests and do something for others get my hands dirty but that's all right he understands the condescending bastard

§

To start the morning off there was an envelope in the mail the mailman comes bright and early to our place I opened it to find a rejection slip from a little magazine in Toronto a magazine with a circulation of two hundred and they turn down my poems with a pretentious printed rejection slip and not a word of comment as if I wasn't already grouchy enough as I set out for the slums I was wearing an old pair of corduroys and a sweatshirt and my heavy cowhide coat in the freezing cold breathing like a steam engine as I got on the bus the corner of Clark and Pine and headed west along Pine with winter people bundled in the seats around me changing buses at Cote des Neiges Road down the hill getting off at Dorchester and Guy then the number 78 to Notre Dame still holding onto my transfer because believe it or not I had to take yet another bus that meant four buses to get me there they weren't just waiting for me either like the pony express every transfer meant stomping my feet on the frozen ground jumping up and down waiting staring along the street hands in pockets mouth fuming like a dragon scowling and cursing at James the phony and thinking I was stupid as hell to do this there are do-gooders and do-badders and do-nothingers and I thought it was good enough to be the last of these I didn't get any special kick out of helping the helpless that was for certain types like James who'd walk across the North Pole to help someone and if everyone was happy and contented James wouldn't know what to do with himself he'd waste away from misery like a doctor who profits off the disease and pain of others a cop a fireman if everything was going well they'd have no place in life but why did James have to get me into this I'm the kind born to help out by contributing money anonymously or even openly if I had money it was that simple all James had to do was wait a few years and perhaps I'd get rich somehow just like that you never could tell meanwhile I was freezing on the corner of Notre Dame and Guy and supposed to visit some oldtimer and help clean and paint his apartment when I could be home working on my poem my new poem the long one that needs so much work me being the slow but sure type unlike whats-his-name guy at Intercourse another magazine that rejected me guy writes seven or eight a day *he says* not that anyone believes him or notices him either I take my time my poems tight and taut unlike a lot of people I know

The sun by now up and bulging with brilliance but not doing much to warm the city it was nine-thirty and another thing that rat James I had to get up at eight o'clock "just this one day" sure but if I lose the day it upsets everything I'll be worn the hell out not able to get anything done in the evening and maybe tomorrow probably I'll wake at eight that's the way my body works and won't be able to get back to sleep that will piss me off no end because I can't start work that early waking at nine is just right I make my coffee and Diane is already gone to her job and I'm alone in the apartment where it's warm locked in from the bitter outdoors take a shower make my coffee and in my old wool housecoat sit at the desk and get myself ready get the lines out I'm up to four pages now the longest poem I've done yet trying to avoid thinking about outside things I wouldn't admit this to anyone but when you get that far along and you think it might be a major work little thoughts creep in and you have to keep them out until the work is finished because they might interfere with the flow like I'm thinking of well I suppose I would submit this for the President's Medal that is if I get it published but Christ surely anyone will see how good thinking too of the Tamarack Review might as well try it there start at the top my thoughts always turning this way except I put them out of my mind best I can when at my desk it takes a while then it starts to come the right word the line the movement the sound it's all got to be right Christ I must write each line I don't know how many times it's a pursuit of perfection is what it is and now here I am down in the slums standing across from the Salvation Army an old tavern at my back it's not ten in the morning and guys going into the tavern Christ two men in their thirties one with a light windbreaker on and his shirt half

unbuttoned and his chest bare to the piercing air and
the other guy in a dirty red and white leather jacket
pantlegs tucked into work boots they duck into the
tavern and across the street a couple of old women
climb the steps to the Sally Ann next time I see when
I see James I'm going to tell him to go fuck himself the
hairs of my nose are stiffened stomping my feet at
least my feet haven't frozen yet and to make it worse
I've got to buy the goddamn groceries sometime today
and get that print that Diane wants when am I going
to do that I'm not going to stay down here all day I'll
do my bit and clear out I think my hair is frozen
dammit I never go outside this early my hair still damp
from showering it feels like the ends are frozen I'll
probably get my hair full of paint too and that'll be
lovely that arsehole James why do I know guys like
him why didn't I tell him emphasize how important
this work was I was doing when's that goddam bus
coming it's I've been standing here fifteen minutes
almost and

And that other bastard John fuck him too
another of these holy frauds I should tell him to paint
the bloody place himself boy I'm fuming I'm frozen
right through

Minutes like hours later the bus moseying
down the street coming slowly from the east taking its
time the driver getting a big kick out of the human
icicles standing at the stops ahead of him three women
and a short little man waiting with me the women
digging tickets out of their purses as the bus draws up
I was there first but I let them get on ahead of me

that's my good turn for the day now I can go home I'm shivering my feet getting numb the windows of the bus frosted over some of them with little peepholes where passengers rubbed their bare hands on the frost to melt it off I figure I'd better do the same so I'd know when I got to this place some old Mr. Benoit crippled with arthritis about eighty years old lives by himself in some dump and James said it would help to clean it up and paint it there was going to be another guy graduate student from McGill not much of an apartment said James hardly more than one room in fact just a tiny room with a tiny kitchen and bathroom the old man neither drank nor smoked James said he couldn't afford to he'd been living there about fifteen years by himself and the apartment had deteriorated if it was ever anything to begin with and it probably wasn't just clean it up and paint it James said and I asked how long it would take I never painted anything in my life and he said John will show you he's into social work of course he'll show you get it started while you're doing cleaning he has the stuff he'll have everything there

Sounds like a lot of work to me I said

It won't take long a few hours dig in get at it a matter of hours

Well if that's all

The bus took its time passing the little grocery and beer stores and taverns and hole-in-the-wall snack bars and rundown old brick buildings and ragged kids out playing in the side streets I checked the piece of paper again with the address and directions when I got close I pulled the cord and got off and walked half a block and crossed the street and went down a side street a ways to get to it

Low crumbling attached buildings squeezed in between a black warehouse and abandoned ironworks factory waiting to be demolished the other side of the street a long high wooden fence with the sign Creary's Lumber Yard the old guy's address a squat little building the front marked over by kids crayons and chalk a moth-eaten curtain showing through the frost on the ground floor window no other curtains in any other windows cars parked along the street I look around for this John's panel truck it's five to ten I'm five minutes early but the bastard should be here have the work half done by now what kind of do-gooder is he the bus ride hasn't taken the frost out of my bones I stand on the sidewalk shivering then walk up and down boots squeaking on the hard snow what do I do now go in start sweeping floors where is that prick maybe he didn't bring the truck might've come in a car or maybe parked around the corner or in an alley took a taxi the rotten bastard I should have worn a heavy sweater I can't stand out here all day maybe the old sonuvabitch'll give me a cup of coffee maybe that John character is already in there that'd be great now if I stood out here freezing to death waiting for him and he was inside all the time

I approach the door try to look in through the glass all covered with thick furry frost I can't see a thing no bell so I knock I knock gently knuckles brittle from the cold my gloves thin the paint on the door rough and jagged I'm afraid to rap on the frosty glass it might break I hammer with the side of my hand like a karate fighter it still hurts and a thought jumps into my head *I could go away now*

I'd showed up I'd done my bit the old gaffer's probably away somewhere independent proud hates condescending patronizing bourgeois do-gooders locked his door went out to visit a friend or something

James look I'll say indignant as hell you get me up and out in the cold I go there and not only your friend John he's nowhere in sight but there's nobody home

But

In my head I hear James answering but he *was* home and John got there on time at ten

Like hell he did I say there was no truck and I was at the place at ten

My watch now at one-minute-to-ten if I take off now I don't want to run into John just showing up as I'm leaving

And that old guy I knocked and knocked and almost knocked the door down and broke my fist almost knuckles all bloody if he was there why didn't he answer I couldn't stand around all day at his door I must've been ten minutes trying to get in and nobody answered I figured he'd forgot about us coming or didn't want us so he was out or in there hiding I got frozen stiff I wasn't going to wait around for your friend John and if he was on time then either his watch or mine wasn't working and mine keeps good time so I said what the hell I was really mad I went all that way to help some old fucker and I was just wasting my time

But I'm telling you he *was* there he just didn't hear your knock he's an old man his hearing's not good John's there with him he called me about noon wondering where you were I know you can't go down now

You're damn right I can't

Outraged as hell

I'll talk to John this evening James saying find out how he got in he didn't mention any problem I wonder what happened I'll call you after I've talked to him

Well maybe the old man came back from wherever he was or woke up or something I don't know anyway all I know is my hand hurts maybe a bone broken if you don't think I knocked hard enough

Later he calls again and says I talked to John and he says you must have been knocking at the outside door because there's a little hallway inside and the old man's apartment there's two apartments in there one unoccupied and the old man's and there's two inside doors

I didn't know that how could I the windows were covered with frost

Didn't you try the outside door? It was open all you had to do was turn the knob and walk in and knock at the inside door

Or maybe it wasn't open

I'm looking at it now the knob and glance up the street but no panel truck coming it's ten o'clock on the nose

John said he might have been one or two minutes late because of the traffic but not more

One or two minutes maybe one minute if that door was open I could turn the knob and then well I've got a conscience I mean I believe the old man's not here or doesn't want us I mean that's a legitimate reason for not hanging around but if this door if it's locked well hell that's it I mean that's it I'm getting the hell out of here but if it's open

Well I never thought of trying the door James it never occurred to me it looked locked I mean you don't just walk into someone's place like that I was thinking it was his own door it looked like it the house only small I didn't think anyone else lived there and why in Christ's name wasn't John on time or even early he should've known I don't know anything about this kind of stuff

I'm shivering feeling a rotten anticipation of going inside and grubbing around cleaning up some filthy hole I mean that's a government thing that's why social agencies exist that's work that's employment for some people everyone complaining about unemployment and now they expect me for nothing to go clean up some lousy apartment that should be torn down not cleaned up or else fixed up by someone who knows what he's doing and getting paid for it Christ I write poems that's enough work to do for free now I'm supposed to go cleaning up the slums while the fat cats in the government drive their limousines and pad their bank accounts in Switzerland what in hell are taxes for

I started to break away and take off the urge almost irresistible because time was flying and that panel truck any minute might come and this last escape route would be closed look at that frost in the windows not only the door window but the front window off to the side that house must be like a deep freeze inside I can see me scrubbing floors and painting walls with my big coat on bloody misery okay I know that old guy lives in it all the time but that's the system it's got to be fixed up here I am I'd just be perpetuating it by contributing the minimum aid keeping the important and necessary things from getting done that's a social problem that has to be legislated against I don't want to be like some nobleman coming down to the poor once a year pretending to help them and getting a good feeling that doesn't help it only allows these conditions to exist I shouldn't be here I'm never going to thaw out

I put my hand on the doorknob surely to God he wouldn't leave his front door open my heart stepping up its beat the street one-way south I'd walk briskly because I had to get warm find a little restaurant and have a coffee and thaw out then take the bus uptown and do that shopping and get home and see what could be salvaged from a fruitless adventure

The knob turns and the door opens and my spirit sinks I'd forgotten almost I might actually go in there straining to make a getaway down the street almost out of it my resolution crumbling away in the face of a way out oh hell

I can still close the door I stick my head inside it's dark as night suddenly the stench hits me like a fist in the face as if the floor is covered with decaying bodies or decades of garbage piled up pulsating with maggots in the cold air the odor petrified and ghastly something scurrying across the floor like a darker shadow I remember a thing I read in a newspaper in the summer some high school kids a grant from the government go into the slums and help out the poor not unlike anyway and the kids said they were amazed at what they found one place they went the apartment crawling with cockroaches were like a moving carpet on the floor and all over the kitchen table and the sink and the dishes and the old couple who lived there when they ate the roaches crawled over the food and they just shook them off before taking a bite this'd be the same thing this is the kind of rundown dump and it's an old man with no hope for a long time and the wildlife of the slum have taken over and was I supposed to go in and confront cockroaches and rats and mice and spiders for a day in the middle of the freezing cold of winter I jump as a rat or mouse runs across the floor jump with fright and repulsion and the smell almost making me gag I know by God this isn't the spot for me I'll think about it later my reaction so immediate you couldn't say I thought about it body spirit brain reacting as one no reasoning matters out reaching a more noble self-sacrificing decision whatever it might be but one instant of total revulsion closing the door a quick look up the street and at my watch one minute after ten well John wasn't showing that's it beating a retreat down the street almost running thinking maybe the old guy was dead yeah no point sprucing a place up for a dead man a final look around have to know if the truck arrived if John saw me something nosing around the corner at Notre Dame but never mind I turn my own corner walking rapidly out of sight now an enormous sense of relief and a few other feelings but when you think about it I'm right I'll do what I can when opportunity presents itself in the future support sweeping social reform you have to do these things from the top for me to paint walls in some cruddy hovel a lot of good that would do

Lennie's Girl

It is now February. I hate my job. I hate the place I live in. I dream of sunny Spain, of palm trees, sitting in cafes drinking cheap wine, good wine but cheap. Since I have to be frugal I've been living in an awful basement room on Saint Jacques near Atwater. My building is in a row of gray tenements which look much better outside than they are inside, though they don't look so great outside either. I get this room for seven dollars a week, it comes complete with fridge, sink, cockroaches and crazy people. The man next door is an insane drunk who a few nights ago chased his wife out into the snow in her nightdress. Two cops brought her back and did their best to smooth out the family quarrel. Then there's the janitor and his wife. But never mind. When you're saving money you're supposed to put up with this kind of thing. I'm not sure if it's really that much of a saving. I've gotten so I drink myself numb every night in order to tolerate the roaches and everything else about this depressing place and though I buy the cheapest wine it still costs money. I've been thinking of moving.

This is a story about a girl named Irene. Irene works in the office of the chemical plant where I'm a lab assistant. I make forty-five dollars a week.

Irene is quite pretty, she's got a big set of... breasts. A big set of tits. Her legs are a little heavy but you don't notice that.

I myself am not such a bad looking fellow and I am hardly what you'd call stupid. I know a few things and I've also got a sense of humour. But—I think this is the worst fault in the world especially when it comes to getting women—I seem to be very shy, very shy and self-conscious. I think I was born that way. I act like a bumbler and a stumbler, you know, and I have a hard time looking a girl or anyone in the eye, and I blush easily, and I never know what to say. I could be exaggerating this but if I'm not all that bad I still feel that I am. I know it shows too, I can tell by the way people look at me.

Irene is the opposite, she's easy mannered and unself-conscious and friendly with everyone—and it's because of that I thought we might hit it off. She could complement me, so to speak, make all the small talk, see that there were no embarrassing silences, help me make my moves when I was too timid. I didn't come right out and think this, but as I see it now that's what I was looking for.

Not such a long time ago she said, "Hi." She was still at her desk cleaning up and I was leaving for home, walking through the office.

"Hi," I said.

"Do you work in the lab?"

"Yes."

"What's your name'?"

"Lennie."

"I mean your full name."

"Oh. Lennie Corcoran. Leonard Corcoran."

She shuffled through some papers. "Here it is. Here's your T4 slips."

"Oh. Thanks."

That was our first encounter. After that she said hello to me whenever I walked by. The way her smile flashed I thought, "I think she likes me. I think I'll ask her out."

I wasn't living a total hermit's life. On weekends I'd go to a movie or a coffeehouse or a pub, and sometimes I'd go with my lab-mates Gagnon and Smythe and get drunk. I needed some diversions like this or I'd go out of my mind. So even if I hadn't done it yet it was not out of the question for me to take a girl out, providing she didn't have expensive tastes.

It took me a few weeks to work myself up to asking her, and when I finally did it was a miracle that I got through it. I would have changed my mind at the last second except I wasn't quick witted enough to think of an alternative reason for stopping at her desk in such a sweat. My voice was dry and shaking as I spoke. On my face was a twisted smile designed to show I was performing a casual everyday act, my debonair smile. Of course it must have looked pitiful.

"Um... Irene... um... " That was the first time I'd called her by name. To my amazement she responded to it, to that peculiar sound that escaped my throat.

She looked up at me smiling. "Um... ah... listen, I, uh... you wouldn't... you don't suppose... well, what I mean to say is, would you like to—would you come out—like to go—Friday night, come out with me?"

"Friday night?"

"Well, if you're busy, it doesn't matter—I mean—"

I could see her thinking. Then she said, "Sure, I'd love to."

"Oh? Oh. Good. Listen, uh... we'll... like what would be, let's see now... Friday night... "

"Do you know where I live?"

"No—no, I don't, no—"

She told me her address and said why didn't I call for her at nine on Friday night. She gave me another smile and I moved my mouth into the shape of what I supposed would be a smile of my own. I left quickly, my legs wobbling, hardly able to support me.

I very pointedly avoided seeing her the rest of the week. I was afraid to risk a conversation. I didn't want to ruin things, I didn't want to be found out. It was impossible for me to act like a normal human being in front of a pretty girl.

On Friday evening it would not be so bad, I told myself, because whatever else we did we would have something to drink, and that would fortify me.

§

Immediately after work Friday I went with Smythe and Gagnon to Marriot's Tavern. Marriot's is in the midst of a lot of factories and naturally does a flourishing business. Smythe eats there every day and Gagnon who has a wife and three small children about twice a week, but for myself I feel I can afford it only once every two weeks, on pay day. Other days I bring my lunch and eat it in the lab, always the same lunch, one baloney sandwich and one peanut butter sandwich.

Sometimes on Friday the spirit of the weekend is too much for me. I awake Saturday morning remembering vaguely that I stayed with the boys at the tavern and later, at some point, we took a cab uptown and visions of shoddy nightclubs on the Main pass through my head, bar girls and strippers and low coloured lights, loud bands, drunken talk, and countless pints of beer. I examine my wallet and count the change in my pocket, and with a little calculation discover there's five or six dollars missing. The reason it's not more is because of Gagnon. After a certain stage in the night it's impossible to pay for your own drink, he insists on picking up all bills. Once he's had a few in him he acts like a free-spending millionaire. But I don't want to start talking about Gagnon. Nor about Smythe. This has nothing to do with them.

"I've got to go," I said, after four beers. "I'm taking a girl out tonight."

"A girl! What girl? Tell us about her," said Gagnon.

"You don't know her," I said.

"What's she look like?"

"Not bad. I've seen worse."

172

"Has she got a friend?" said Smythe. "I'm not doing anything this evening."

"Has she got two friends?" said Gagnon.

"Naw, she's got no friends, she's all by herself."

"Did you fuck her yet?" said Gagnon.

Such a question made me embarrassed. Smythe laughed.

"I just met her," I said.

"Where'd you meet her'?"

"Oh... I don't know, just somewhere, I forget."

"Ah! Ah! There's something funny here. I bet you we know her."

"Is she from the plant? One of the office girls?"

"I don't have time for these stupid questions, I've got to get moving." I swallowed the last mouthful of beer.

"Tell us about it Monday, we'll want to hear everything," said Gagnon. He stuck his tongue out in a point and wiggled it around. "Don't forget what they like!"

I had about a twenty minute walk to my rooming house. It was dark outside and a few snowflakes were beginning to fall. I walked quickly, crossing the bridge over the frozen Lachine Canal. My walk took me past factories and warehouses and rundown tenement houses, along gloomy little streets, then over the railroad tracks and past a two-spired church and on up to Saint Jacques.

§

She lived away on Van Horne and I took a bus to get there but when I rang her buzzer and she came down I hailed a taxi, not wanting to look like a cheapskate. It was still snowing.

"Where are we going?" she said. In the back seat of the cab I felt the touch of her coat against mine.

"Oh, well, we'll go—I don't know—we'll go downtown, go to a club somewhere or something. What do you want to do?"

"It's up to you."

"We can—Oh, I don't know—we can go to the *Catastrophe* and have a beer, I mean a drink—"

"All right." Then she said, "Would you like to go to a party later? I know where there's one."

"A party? Oh, sure, fine. Sure, why not? Where?"

What if I'd made definite plans, had somewhere I'd really wanted to take her? But I didn't know what we were to do that evening. She was the first girl I'd asked out since coming to Montreal. Vaguely I thought we would visit a few clubs and drink and dance and talk and get to know each other and then I'd take her home, and who knows what then?

We were silent most of the way downtown. I was sure it wasn't bothering her, the silence, that she could make conversation if she wished or she could just as easily say nothing. I sat beside her trying to get my mind to revolve so I could think up something brilliant to say. But all I could think of saying was, "It's snowing quite hard," and I wasn't about to say something as stupid as that. I squirmed, wishing the taxi would go faster so we could get to the Catastrophe and have a drink and my brain might unseize itself. I glanced at her out of the corner of my eye, I could make her out in the twilight of the cab, her long flowing hair, her straight little nose, the bulge of her coat where her breasts were. This is me here, I thought, I'm taking this gorgeous girl out, she's with me, not with someone else. It was almost enough to make me panic. Could I handle it, was I capable of pulling it off, would she not realize that a mistake's been made, that I had outreached myself, that I was bluffing? I'll be cool, I instructed myself, I'll act cool and possibly a little superior. I'm the one, it's me who's disdained to make small talk, not her, I'm merely sitting here with important things on my mind and the girl is of minor significance in my life, just another pretty face that I'm passing an evening with. It's all a matter of attitude.

"I've never been to the *Catastrophe*," she said.

"What? Oh. Oh, you haven't?"

"No."

"Well... " That must call for some further comment. But what can you say? After all, she only made a statement. So she hasn't been to the *Catastrophe*. Am I supposed to say, "I've been there." You could take that for granted.

"It's not bad," I said. "It's just a place." That's exactly what it was, a place, a bar, a club. You've seen one you've seen them all. "It's got funny pictures—drawings on the wall," I said. But how could I describe them? I'd only begin and then my description would break down because I don't have the gift for describing things in a way to make people laugh. And if the pictures were funny, then my description should be funny. "You'll see when we get there."

The taxi cost me two sixty-five plus a ten cent tip. Irene didn't see my little tip, and the driver, he'd never see me again. Two seventy-five. I ate beans and baloney every day for a week to save that much.

The *Catastrophe* is above the Royal Tavern, you go up two flights of steep stairs where there's a coat check and a tray with a quarter stuck to it to show how much you're supposed to tip. "We might as well keep our coats with us, we'll only be here a few minutes," I said. Luckily there was no waiter or bouncer around just then waiting to show us to a table with his palm outstretched. Taking advantage of the opportunity I quickly hustled Irene to a table. I helped her off with her coat and draped it over the back of her chair. It was dark, there were no electric lights, only red candles in netted globes on the center of each table. There was a low stage against one wall and on the wall were the funny drawings I'd mentioned. They were drawings of weird looking people playing musical instruments, and what made them most weird was that they had feet for hands and hands for feet. You'd have to see them for yourself.

A girl in black tights waited on us. "What'll you have?" I said to Irene.

"I'd like a zombie."

I ordered a beer for myself. When the girl brought them she said, "That'll be two fifty, please."

"Two fifty?"

I paid, looking at Irene's tall fancy drink with disgust. I wanted her to get feeling good but by God not at these prices. It was all I could do to restrain myself from remarking how much that zombie cost. What the hell, I thought, it's only money. When I get to know her better I'll tell her she should drink beer.

"How is it?" I said, trying to grin.

"It's nice. Those are the pictures you meant?" she said, looking at the stage. "They *are* funny."

"Yeah." I made a sound something like a laugh. I took a deep drink of my beer. I knew the beer cost seventy-five cents, an outrageous price in itself, so that meant her drink had cost a buck seventy-five. I vowed never to come to this place again. I poured the last of my bottle into my glass and when the head subsided took another big drink. It was ice cold and punishing on the throat. I was shaking like hell inside. I took another big drink and it was all gone. "I think I'll have another one," I said.

"Already?"

"I was thirsty." A feeble smile. I certainly wasn't going to wait until she was finished and order two of the same. It wasn't economical. That zombie was the sum total for her as far as I was concerned. As long as she sipped it slow I could keep ordering beer and get feeling good and when she finished we could leave.

When my second pint came I found myself nervously devouring it rapidly again. I should have been getting relaxed but I wasn't.

"Were you born in Montreal?" she said.

"No. I'm from New Brunswick. I came up here in the fall. What about you? Are you from here?"

"No, I'm from Winnipeg."

"Oh? How long have *you* been here?"

"A little over two years."

"How do you like it?"

"It's all right. I like it. There's more going on than in Winnipeg."

"Yeah, that's right."

You can see we were doing some talking, not just sitting there silently.

I wondered how old she was. I considered asking her, but didn't know whether I should or not. She was probably about twenty. I'd ask her later, I thought.

"Smoke?" I said, rattling my package open.

"Thank you." I lit it for her.

"This, uh, party, what time—I mean what time should, will we go there? Where is it?" She'd already told me but in my distraction it hadn't registered.

"It's not far from here. It's on Aylmer. We can go anytime, whenever you like."

"Okay. There's no hurry, I suppose."

I couldn't stop avoiding her eyes. I would look at her when she spoke and then when I replied I would look at her arm, or at the table, or at the next table. This is a nervous habit of mine and I know I should do something about it. It's not as if I don't know I'm doing it.

In the corner of the club, to the right of the stage, there were musical instruments, a piano, drums, a saxophone and a bass. In a while four musicians appeared and began playing dance numbers. Several couples got up from their tables and began dancing on the stage.

"Would you, ah, like to dance?" I said.

"Not right now," she said.

"Oh? Okay. I don't feel like it now myself. I just thought I'd ask."

She smiled.

I ordered another beer, drank it, getting filled up with gas inside, trying to slip out a few silent burps, and when I was about to order my fourth I said, generously, "You must be finished that drink by now. Do you want another one? Or something else?" Like, maybe a beer, I felt like saying. But I was getting a little better now, a little more calm, a little more powerful. I could see she'd almost finished her drink. I could scarcely avoid inviting her to have another.

"All right," she said.

"The same thing'?"

She thought a moment. Maybe she took pity on me. "No, I think I'll have a gin and tonic instead."

"It turned out that she saved me fifty cents.

"Who's having this party?" I said, shouting over the music.

"Some friends."

"From at work'?"

"Pardon?"

"Are they from at work?"

"No. I used to share an apartment with the girl who's having it."

"Oh."

The music stopped and the musicians took another break. The stage emptied, shadowy couples returned to their tables.

"How do you like working at the plant?" I said.

"It's all right. I don't mind."

"I don't like it, I mean my job. I'm not going to be there long."

"No?"

"I'm quitting in the summer. I'm pulling out."

"Oh?"

"I'm heading for Spain."

"Spain? That sounds nice."

"I've got a friend there, a guy from school. It's a great place, beaches, no snow, everything's cheap. Have you ever been to Europe?"

"No."

"Do you ever think of going?"

"Oh, sometimes, I've thought about it, maybe someday."

"I bet you'd like it."

"Maybe."

There was a change coming over me. The beer which I had throttled down was catching up with me. It may have been the dimness of the place too because I get drunk easier in a dark place. My head was starting to swim. It wasn't unpleasant but I had the sensation I might possibly lose control of myself if I didn't slow down. I suddenly wanted to say something like, "Hey, you're really beautiful!" I almost did. I caught my tongue in time. Something told me I had to think it over first. It would sound awful funny, coming from me especially. I had a strong urge to bend near her and kiss her. Her mouth looked wide and soft, her cheeks cool, smooth, her hair flowing and glittering. It would be nice to touch her. I started to move but my muscles didn't respond. Don't be a fool, something in me said. But I should, it's probably the best thing to do. But how would she react? If she pushed you away—what if she got mad? It's not wise to move too quickly. You don't want to look like you're getting drunk. I continued to look at her, the urge to hold her welling up in my chest.

"You'll have to send me a card from Spain," she said.

"Sure. I sure will." Perhaps I shouldn't have told her about Spain. She would realize now that I wasn't going to be around for long and there was no future in becoming involved with me.

"Of course I won't stay there forever," I said. "Maybe only six months or so. Maybe you can come over and visit me."

She just smiled.

"It doesn't make sense, you know, people are stupid working all the time," I said recklessly. "They're like slaves, they don't enjoy themselves, they're all trying to pay for houses and cars and all kinds of junk they don't need. They're like squirrels in a cage, going like mad and staying in the same spot... What do you think?"

"I don't know. Somebody's got to work. We can't all lie in the sun and do nothing."

"I don't mean lying around on a beach every day. I mean travelling, going to strange places, seeing the world."

"Oh."

The dance music started again. This time I really felt like dancing. I started to get up. "Would you like to dance?" I said.

"I think we'd better go now. We don't want to be late for the party."

"Oh. Oh, okay. That's right, the party."

As parties go it was the usual lousy way to waste time. I don't know if I've ever enjoyed a party in my life. When we got there we could hear the noise soon as we stepped out of the elevator. It was another of those eyesore high-rise buildings. The hall was plushly carpeted and rock music was blasting from apartment 907 and there was a crowd of voices talking and laughing and shouting. We were let in by someone near the door. The lights were low and bodies were standing tightly together, there was hardly room to move around. Further in I saw a lot of motion where dancing was going on. The air was thick with cigarette smoke.

"Hi, Irene! Put your coat in the bedroom. In here."

We squeezed our way through an army of bodies, mostly male, and reached the relative peace of the bedroom. The wide double bed was buried under a mountain of coats. The girl who'd let us in was tiny and lively. "He's here,"she said meaningfully to Irene.

Irene flushed slightly. "This is Lennie," she said.

"Oh. Hi, Lennie." It was as if she hadn't seen me until now.

"Hi," I said, trying to find a place to put my coat where I could locate it again.

"This is Louise. We used to have an apartment together on Lincoln," said Irene.

"The drinks are in the kitchen."

We fought our way to the kitchen where the sink was a sloppy mess of glasses and bottles and ashtrays. There was a large basin of ice cubes and a variety of bottles: Beefeater, Smirnoff's, Seagram's, Canadian Club, Johnny Walker. They were all opened and about half were already empty. There were quarts of mix, bitter lemon, coke, ginger ale, seven-up. A few sodden cigarette butts lay at the bottom of the sink. Everywhere there were empty beer bottles. A couple of guys in suits were fussing around pouring themselves drinks. I looked in the fridge, there were about six dozen pints of Molson's and Labatt's stacked inside and nothing else. It was the same old picture. I was undecided whether to keep drinking beer or take advantage of the hard stuff which I could never afford for myself. I shut the fridge door. "What'll you have?" I said to Irene. They say you aren't supposed to mix your drinks, it will make you sick, but I don't know if I believe that. I've gotten sick just by drinking too much beer and nothing else.

"A gin and tonic," she said.

I mixed a strong one for her and one of the same for myself. She tasted it. "Ooh, that's too strong. Put some more tonic in it." I did, then we started wading our way to the livingroom. We were crushed together going through a narrow hall and her hair brushed my face. "Who's 'he'?" I said.

"What?"

"Who's 'he'?"

"What do you mean?"

"What that girl said, she said, 'He's here.' "

"Oh, that. I don't know what she meant."

Ha! She didn't know!

It wasn't too long before 'he' made his presence known, I could tell soon as I saw him approaching. He was looking at Irene and she was pretending not to see him. I could have described him before I saw him, tall, easy mannered, very smartly dressed and I suppose what some people would call handsome, although it was not a word I would use to describe him. Slimy would have been closer. "Hi, Irene, I haven't seen you since... for a long time."

"Oh?" She had not said "Oh?" like that to me. I could tell she was looking into his eyes.

"Let's dance."

"All right."

Giving only the faintest nod my way Irene moved off with him. I clenched my drink. With slitted eyes I followed their movement on the crowded floor. They danced closely together, they were waltzing even though the music was fast and everyone else was wriggling and shaking and not touching. What goddamn nerve, what rotten nerve that guy had.

All she had to do was say, "No thanks, I'm with someone." If it was only one dance even—but they stayed together for twenty minutes on the floor while I stood lost on the sidelines drinking and smouldering and feeling lousy and hateful as hell.

She must have mentioned at some point that I was her escort, because later he brought her back to where I was and soulfully tore his eyes away from hers and moved on. His glance for a moment had fallen over me the same way you'd look at a chair.

I didn't say anything to her.

"Did you see my drink'?" she said after a moment.

"No." It was on the windowsill but I wasn't going to tell her.

"I wonder where it is."

I wanted to say it's not up your ass or you'd feel it. But I just said, "I imagine where you left it."

She looked at me. "Are you mad at me?"

"Me? Of course not. What for?"

"Paul... Paul's an old friend. We used to be quite good friends."

"You don't say."

"I really had to dance with him, I could hardly have refused."

I didn't say anything.

"I guess I'll get another drink," she said. She started away. I stood there a second, then went after her. "I'll get it for you," I said. What the hell, I didn't own her, she could do what she wanted, so it was an old boyfriend, so what?

"Thanks."

I brought back her drink, getting myself another one while I was at it.

When some slow music came on I asked her to dance. I prefer slow music, I don't want to be out there on the floor jumping around like a monkey. I never dance to the fast stuff if I can help it. A slow waltz is intimate, it makes more sense for a man and a woman to dance that way. The other is like an exhibition you could do by yourself, you don't need a partner.

Imitating her boyfriend's words and manner I said, "Let's dance," but she didn't notice the sarcasm.

"Okay."

I put the drinks on the windowsill near her old glass and we edged our way onto the floor and—and to be blunt it was like dancing with a post, she stayed stiffly away from me and I almost strained my arm keeping her as close as I did. I felt her hair on my face but not her cheek. Her large breasts touched against me and for a moment I started to get a little excited but it took me no more than a moment to sense her remoteness from me, and the stirring subsided. I didn't say anything to her. I would have had to shout anyway because of the volume of the music. When it ended whoever was handling the records put on some ear-splitting screaming and shouting by the Grand Funk Railroad or someone and I said, "The hell with that." She stood there looking at me quizzically, all she could see was my mouth moving. I made a gesture of resignation and led her off the floor. "Don't like that song!" I shouted at her.

Then some other creep came over and asked her to dance. She looked at me this time, she probably didn't know the guy, and I shrugged. She went onto the floor and the two of them were soon squirming and shaking like all the rest of the couples. She was laughing and seemed to be enjoying it. I had, I suppose, a kind of envy of them all out there. They weren't self-conscious about their movements or the expressions on their faces. "A bunch of dummies," I said to myself. "I really hate these stupid parties. I'm going to leave soon even if I have to go alone. Piss on her."

"Do you like these parties?" I said when she returned.

"I guess so. Sure."

"They bore me. I find them a pain in the ass."

She didn't say anything.

"Do you want to stay long?" I said.

"Why, don't you?"

"Naw, I don't think so. I don't know anybody here. It's too crowded, it's too smokey, it's too noisy. These parties are all alike. When do you want to leave?"

"I don't know. Whenever you like."

"Okay. Let's finish our drinks and go. We can go down to the Swiss Hut, it's only down the street."

"No, I'd rather go home."

We went into the bedroom and dug out our coats. Suddenly she dropped hers and said, "Just a minute, I'll be right back." She disappeared through the door. I stood there with my coat in my hand. Then I put it on and waited. I went to the bedroom window and looked out. In the night the city lights were everywhere, we were up high enough that you could see quite far, apartment buildings lit up, streetlights, car lights, skyscraper lights, lights on the Jacques Cartier Bridge, everything but stars. "What's she doing?" I wondered. I thought she was going to the bathroom but surely she had enough time by now... It was hot standing there in my heavy winter coat. "Christ!" I was getting mad. I squeezed my way out through the bedroom door to look for her. It was difficult to pick someone out in the dim light and with so many people jammed together. I pushed between bodies squeezing by like I was made of elastic. All that effort for what? In a little open space in the corner of the room that guy with his arms around Irene, the two of them clinging together like long lost lovers, and they were kissing. Never mind. I bulled my way back to the bedroom pushing people out of the way, then in the bedroom I decided to leave by myself and started out again. No, that wasn't the thing to do, I couldn't run off like that, what would I say when I saw her at work? When she asked me where I went, and why, what could I tell her? What if word got around to Smythe and Gagnon? In the sober morning I would look ridiculous. The night had to end on better terms, preferably on my terms. If nothing else, if there was only some way I could humiliate her... A crazy thought like that going through my head. In a sense I felt quite

capable now, quite strong, there was no danger of my
being self-conscious, I was too burned up, I didn't need
to make a good impression, there was nothing to be
gained and nothing to be lost. Finally she returned,
flushed and breathless. "I'm sorry I was so long," she
said.

"I'm leaving now. Are you coming or staying?"

She gave me another one of those quizzical
looks. As though it was me who was behaving oddly.
Here she was making a fool out of me, treating me like
an idiot, and when I didn't like it she acted as if I was
being abrupt and sullen for no reason in the world.

"What do you mean?" she said. "Of course I'm
coming. I just wanted to say goodbye to Louise."
Goodbye to Louise, it was.

"Yeah. Well let's go." She put her coat on
without my help which I didn't offer.

Outside the snow was still falling, but lightly.
We plodded along the unplowed sidewalk to
Sherbrooke street. I don't know why I didn't say,
"We're taking a bus, I've already spent enough on you
tonight." Or I could have said, "It's your turn to pay the
taxi, I paid it getting here." It shows a character
deficiency on my part that I didn't have the
nerve to refuse to pay for another cab. Already I'd
spent over ten dollars. And what did I stand to get in
return?

In the taxi, after all this time, she began
chattering away without a break about what a good
time she'd had, how many people were there, what her
friend Louise was doing, where they'd met, things they

did together, mutual friends they had, what these friends were doing. Every now and then as she talked she clutched my arm to emphasize a point, or when she said something she thought was funny she leaned against me and laughed. For a long time I didn't say anything except a bored "yeah" every so often, but she seemed in such good spirits and she was no longer ignoring me... perhaps... slowly and gradually... well, I suppose I shouldn't be so narrow and stubborn about things, a little thing like her kissing an old boyfriend. If I had an old girlfriend it might be nostalgic to kiss her when we met after a long time, there'd be nothing wrong in it. I began to thaw. I could be big about things, forgive quickly. After all it was me she was going home with, if there was anything more to it she'd have stayed at the party and let that tall creep take her home. I reminded myself that you can't expect to win a girl all at once, she knew this other guy a lot better than she knew me. But that was in the past.

The meter in the front was ticking and the nickels were adding up. But I had thrown away so much money now a little more was almost painless. I decided on a daring move. She was chattering and we were sitting close together, our coats touching. Go ahead, go on, I urged myself. Although I was fairly drunk I had still not lost my inhibitions. Nothing ventured, nothing gained. What's there to lose? Like a plunge into cold water I jerked my arm up from beside her and put it around her shoulders. I pulled her closer. She didn't resist. There was a sudden halt in her talking but she picked it right up. I was so concen-

The Black Horse Tavern

trated on what I was doing I had no idea what she was saying. I almost burst with triumph. My impulsive move made me giddy. I said, "Is that right? That's very funny. Ha ha." I became responsive and started chattering and laughing myself, almost giggling, I think. Oh boy. I wondered if she was the kind of girl—what was this thing I read, some psychologist, who said "not so long ago when a boy took a girl home they kissed goodnight but now they make love." I thought of Gagnon and Smythe, if they could see me, see what I had my arm around.

I must have really been drunk because one minute I was sitting glum and sulky and the next I was talking and laughing and in my mind thinking how I was going to go about seducing the very girl that I'd been hating so much. You see, it was all because of the way she acted, the moment she was nice to me and appeared to notice I was there beside her I became a warm, generous person. It doesn't take much with me. I thought of her taking her clothes off and my heart almost stopped, then it began racing. Could I do it? What approach would I take? How were these things done? "Well, let's go to bed," the offhanded approach? Or more romantic, "Irene darling, I want to make love to you"? I couldn't picture myself saying that. Maybe she would take care of everything, perhaps she'd say, "Well, let's go to bed", or "Do you want to make love to me?" Oh yes, do I ever. Ah, I know, at least it would be the best way, when we got to her apartment she would say, "Just a minute while I slip into something more comfortable," and when she returned from the bedroom she'd be wearing a sheer negligee that revealed everything. Just thinking about it was almost enough to make me faint. I squeezed her shoulder, certain that my passion was running like electricity through my hand and into her body. She would sense it, she would respond with her own passion. If I were holding her hand she could squeeze back, but it was harder to tell with her shoulder, particularly with her winter coat on. I looked at her profile. She became silent for a moment looking straight ahead. I squeezed her shoulder again. She turned her face and smiled.

When we reached her building I paid the driver, hardly noticing the fare. With trembling hand I tipped him a quarter, eager to get out of the car, throwing my money away, not caring about material matters on a night like this. The cab drove away. Irene was already standing in the foyer out of the snow. I trotted up the walk and opened the outer door and stood before her eagerly, smiling like a fool.

"Well, thanks for a lovely night, I really enjoyed it," she said.

"Oh. Oh yeah. I, uh, I, uh—" What was this? Was she—was I supposed to say, "Aren't you going to invite me in?" Was that the ritual? It must be my move. She wasn't just—

"I'll see you Monday, back at the old job," she said.

There was no time to waste. There was not even time to think. Once she went in the door it was all over. The first thing to do—I grabbed her by both arms and pulled her close. My lips went for hers and when they got there her head was turned slightly and they met her cheek. I released her.

"I have to be getting in now. I'm really tired. Goodnight, and thanks again." She had her key out and was opening the door.

"But—"

"Yes?" she turned. I stared at her helplessly.

"Nothing." What could I say? Whatever I said I would have made a fool of myself, more of a fool than I already was. She gave me the last of her false smiles and disappeared inside. Goddammit all. I left the building, turning towards Cote des Neiges on the chance the buses were still running, my feet leaving a trail behind me in the new snow. I was so mad—mad at her, mad at myself, mad at the world in general—that I almost burst out crying. I trudged through the snow all by myself on the street swearing out loud the longest string of curses you ever heard, but it didn't make me feel any better.

On the Bus

The incident I'm about to relate is of such minor significance that I doubt anyone but myself would bother relating it. I've racked my brain to find a moral behind it. If I found a moral then it would not seem such a waste of time.

One thing about morals is they are always summed up in catchy little phrases like "everybody loves a winner," which to begin with is a lie because I don't love winners. I love losers, failures, flops, non-successes. There is a common bond between flops and myself because I am one, even though I am still a young man. You may consider me too young to be dismissed outright as a flop. Nevertheless I am a flop because I know I'm a flop, and those who consider themselves flops are generally successful at being flops.

I don't want to get too far astray. Aside from establishing an ungainly writing style I've written a paragraph that has little or nothing to do with what I want to say—and in fact I would like to make more irrelevant remarks. My mind wanders badly at all times; I have a deplorable time concentrating. My interest in anything worthwhile, I mean anything that pays dividends as the world understands them, is fleeting at best.

You understand, then, why it is virtually impossible for me to be any kind of success.

Yesterday I learned the horrible truth, namely, that my days as a scholar were over. It was a lovely warm April afternoon, it would have been a nice day for a nice surprise, but this was nineteen seventy-one and not the age of miracles, if ever there was such a time. McGill was teeming with depressingly cheerful drones who had passed their year—but I had failed mine miserably. This news did not come as a surprise to me. How could it have been otherwise when my mind is forever drifting, entertaining daydreams, imaginary love affairs, playing with the lines of a poem, the contours of a painting, scenes from a film, technicolour pictures of myself as a dashingly heroic, imposing, scintillating figure? In reality I am not heroic or scintillating or any of those other words. In appearance I am nondescript—slightly ugly but not enough to draw attention. My mind is not brilliant. I rarely say witty things. I suspect that I am frequently boring the people I talk to.

I can see forming in your mind, Aha, you say, I have this young fellow pegged. He is at heart a romantic, an artist, and he blames himself for failing to pass his courses in engineering which his stern father forced him to take. But you are wrong, my courses were in art and literature—things which interest me although I am unable to *study* them or respond in the proper scholarly tradition. Nor do I have any talent in my own right as an artist of any kind. I am modest, I understand myself—I am a would-be painter, a would-be poet, a would-be film maker, a would-be actor, a would-be singer, and yes, a would-be lover. I do none of these things well nor have I ever given the creative aspect of my life any large attention. I accept what I am: a dilettante, a middle-class dilettante.

I am one with—let me repeat—failures because they remind me of myself. My sympathies go out strongly to them. They are my brothers. We are all destined to muddle along in life. I expect I will succeed at best in holding down some insignificant job throughout my life, using what money I put aside to buy books, the occasional painting, to attend a concert, the movies, to have my small pleasures. I am capable of accepting my condition in reality, even if I continue to allow myself to indulge in fruitless fantasy.

But for all my self-adjustment, to assume I was serene as I walked off the campus of McGill and along noisy Sherbrooke street would be a grave mistake. I had used up my last chance as a student; I could not return to McGill now nor to any other university, because I had failed far too many courses over the past five years. I should have finished in four years and yet I had stumbled on for five, propping myself up with night credits, those I was able to acquire. But now the end had been reached. I had flunked the entire year. They would not take me back. And if I wished to attend another university it would mean sorting out the pieces of the McGill disaster and beginning somewhere even further from the end. This was impossible. It was not just a question of admitting I wasn't cut out to be a scholar, though that was certainly the case; it was a question of money. I could not, I cannot possibly afford to continue as a student. I am more than eight thousand dollars in debt. Over the past five years I've lived on government loans, bank loans, and loans from my family. Very soon I have to start paying this money back. The bank is charging interest, the government will commence doing so if I don't begin paying shortly, and I am morally obliged to repay my father and brother. Neither is wealthy, far from it. They live in Moncton (which I find a depressing city, by the way), where my father is assistant manager of Eaton's rug department and my older brother Ronald a salesman on the same floor. I am the scholar in the family, or was until yesterday. They thought I would do well. I once thought I would do well myself. I *used* to do well, I believe at the age of seventeen I was at my scholarly peak, but towards the end of high school a kind of apathy set in. It was only momentum that carried me off to Montreal and McGill, and that momentum decreased daily until now I am standing still, a scholar *manqué*. I would like to explain why this happened, where this indifference came from, why I just could not give myself to my studies, but I'm not sure I can. It may stem from—I don't know what. I simply don't wish to pursue success, I shy from obligations, I want to have been born rich and able to live the dilettante's life in proper fashion.

You might ask, How could I borrow so much money and leave myself in the position of letting my family down so badly? The answer is this: it's because I enjoyed my life as a student, as a student in the way I was a student. For five years I came and went more or less as I pleased, pausing only now and then to acknowledge the existence of my studies, working only when I absolutely had to in order to extend my way of life. It had to catch up with me. It did so yesterday. Hence, as I said, I wasn't entirely happy as I walked along Sherbrooke with McGill behind me forever. I knew this day had to arrive, the halcyon years end and like my father and brother I would also climb onto the treadmill. Would I work in Eaton's rug department? The thought made me shudder.

I could have berated myself for having been such a loafer, for if I had applied myself I might perhaps have graduated and pursued post-graduate studies and continued as a student possibly all my life. But that was no solution because, to begin with, the academic treadmill is not much different from any other. They expect you to labor over some pointless pursuit, and they're forever looking over your shoulder to see you don't relax. And I would be expected to teach courses and I'd hate that. It was impossible for me to do other than what I did. I could not, for love nor money, apply myself to the degree necessary to succeed. I lived each day for itself. What might happen tomorrow was not my concern.

§

I crossed Peel street and stopped before the windows of the Gallery Martal. There were a few paintings as usual by Bernard Buffet in the window, but that's not why I mention stopping here. My reason is I am going to use a literary device. As I stood before the large window I saw a reflection of my own person.

It was warm yesterday so I wasn't wearing a coat. The month is April (how do authors handle this irksome problem of "is" and "was" when the past is only yesterday?). I was wearing a pair of faded blue jeans and a gray sweatshirt, comfortable clothes but nothing to make you turn your lead. My hair, as is the style, was (is?) shoulder length. These days not only students but even businessmen it seems wear their hair that way. You'll see the implication of my hair later, and how absurd is the incident I am going to describe. Because I'm nearsighted I wear glasses, ordinary wire-rimmed glasses, and I've begun growing a distinguished beard (or what will be such when it's finished). And then there's my size. I am a little over average height and a bit on the portly side. Not much, but perhaps a few pounds overweight as the result of a good appetite and the sedentary life I lead. I have always had an aversion to any exercise aside from walking.

Now that you have my description I can walk away from the windows of Gallery Martal.

It might be safe to say that my earlier remark about the state of my spirits was an understatement. I said I wasn't happy. The truth is, I was distressed, I was depressed. This is understandable because what had I to look forward to? Some manner of drudgery— if I could find it. A perfect case of bitter irony. According to the newspapers employment was scarce, so I would be forced to seek out diligently that which I did not want at all. It was like making the condemned man build his own gallows. I had no idea where I could start. On occasion, during moments of uncommon fortitude and anticipating my present position, I had let my eyes wander over the classified ads in the Montreal Star. I saw many jobs but every one of them made my heart sink. There are no jobs that I know of designed to satisfy persons who do not want to have a job.

As I walked along Sherbrooke, on the bank of a river of roaring traffic, so to speak, I pondered what I could do to make myself feel better. "Doom. Doom lies ahead," I thought. "Tomorrow I walk down a dark corridor at the end of which there is no light. But... that is tomorrow. Today, I will live one last day before giving myself up to slavery."

My bank is at the corner of Sherbrooke and Guy, for I live only one block up the hill on MacGregor. I went into the bank and withdrew a hundred dollars. That left in my account fifty-six dollars and thirty-two cents, not much at all, but then it was part of tomorrow's life, a life of trials and tribulations. Today it could not concern me.

§

No doubt another person in my place would have proceeded to get blindly drunk, that being the traditional course followed by men as hopeless as myself. I do not generally drink but I made a gesture, a somewhat grand gesture in that direction by going directly to the Mountain Street Liquor Store and buying a bottle of champagne.

Let us now glance into the hypothetical future, the immediate future as I pictured it at that moment. You see me thus, several hours later, sprawled languorously in my easy chair at home admiring my new Baeschlen water-colour on the wall, sipping pink champagne, cigarette held lightly in my fingers, while in the background a Chopin *ballade* plays gently on my stereo. From time to time, as the afternoon blends into evening, I rise and go to the kitchen where gradually a meal fit for royalty is coming into existence under the tutelage of my expert fingers...

This, I remind you, was merely the picture I had in my mind. More important, it serves as another literary device, this time to divulge how I spent my hundred dollars.

The painting was the largest extravagance but the easiest to indulge myself in because, of course, a painting is always an investment, isn't it? Although you can never tell with these things. If it's an investment you're making you had better become more acquainted with the artist's contacts than his work. There are many painters around. Karl Baeschlen has no reputation yet, and may never have. But it was because of this I could afford one of his works. I was, I am, much impressed by his talent, splendid pieces of a surrealistic—but stop—this is not important, in fact it has nothing whatever to do with the incident I'm trying to get around to. As far as you are concerned the *size* of the painting is the important thing. It was five feet tall by three feet wide. With frame it cost me sixty-five dollars. As I handed over the money to pay for it there stood beside me on the gallery floor a bag of rather expensive foods carefully selected shortly before from various delicatessens for the sumptuous meal I envisioned. Leaning against the bag of food—which also contained a couple of good Cuban cigars, I might add—was a thin square package which anyone could tell was a long-playing record, though in fact it was two long-playing records (like most romantics I love Chopin, and these were additions to my collection of the works of that great man). And of course there was my bottle of champagne.

My hundred dollars was gone. I could have bought a less expensive Baeschlen, they started at fifty dollars, but then I would not have got the one I wanted. I could also have bought Niagara sparkling wine, which has fizz and bubbles like champagne, but I was not the mood for substitutes.

I now had fifty-six cents in my pocket. This, unfortunately, was insufficient for a taxi home. I was in the Labyrinth Gallery, one of a number of crudely thrown together basement boutiques operated by a collection of young persons, the type some individuals persist in calling "hippies", though I consider the word much out of fashion. However, my views are not always shared by everyone. I know in the minds of some it is still a living word, and serves as a handy generalization. You will see.

The Labyrinth is on Saint Catherine just west of Bleury, almost next door to the Parisien Theatre.

I could, I said to myself, gathering my unwieldy assortment of possessions into my arms, take the Metro to Guy street, then transfer to a bus. But that seemed not the best way, because it meant going through turnstiles and up and down stairs and on and off a subway car as well as a bus. It was simpler, I concluded, to walk down to Dorchester and take one of the three buses that ran along Dorchester turning north at Guy and on up to my street which is MacGregor. It would not be as quick as the Metro, but it would be far easier.

It was not however such a short walk to the nearest stop on Dorchester. The going was extremely awkward, and I had to halt every few paces and adjust my burden. The afternoon had grown quite hot and by the time I reached the bus stop I was perspiring and angry at myself for doing things in what was obviously the wrong way. On the surface I was attempting to make a joyful day of it, but walking around like a pack mule should not have been part of the plot. One day you should try carrying a five-by-three-foot painting, two LP records, a heavy quart of champagne and a bulky bag of groceries as far as I did. Although the bus route was along Dorchester and that was only one block from Saint Catherine, the nearest stop was located in front of Place Ville Marie, another three blocks west.

§

I don't personally know that many elderly people, but if you had asked me what I thought of them as a rule, most probably my reply would have been, "Well, I believe I like them, they're over the hill and not so aggressive, they've seen a good deal of life and I expect they are wiser than they used to be. They are slow moving, I like their pace."

If there's one thing I've always detested it's a person who takes up two seats on a bus.

The scene opens with me climbing onto the number 65 bus with my painting, groceries, records and bottle of champagne. I had my ticket out and ready and with a little flick of thumb and forefinger, the only two parts of my body available, and these only partly so, I dropped the ticket into the slot and sat down. I sat on the long sideseat at the front nearest the door. There was nobody else on this seat which was designed to hold four bodies.

Now that I was seated a casual observer would see me as follows: a young gentleman with records and champagne (both in wrappers) on his lap, an enormous painting (also wrapped but fooling nobody) standing in front of him and hugged in close to his knees, and a large bag of groceries on the seat beside him with a tall loaf of French bread sticking out the top. He had his left hand on this bag keeping it snug against his side.

As the sun glinted off the windows of the skyward-reaching office buildings along Dorchester the bus motored forward stopping at Mansfield, Drummond, Bishop, Guy, then rounding the corner at Guy and travelling northward and upward. Looking out the expansive front windshield I saw ahead the great brick pile of the Montreal General Hospital, assorted towering apartment buildings, a part of the mountain, the busy crossroads at Guy and Saint Catherine. At the different stops we took on new passengers. At Bishop, for example, two oldish women got on and sat on the long seat beside me. They appeared to have just come from a beauty parlour, their gray hair was propped up smartly on their heads, their wrinkled faces were made up carefully with pink powder. They were dressed quite well and they both wore little black gloves. The seat looked like this: the two women, a little space, then me and my supplies squeezed up against the end of the seat. The women sat there sniffing, at any rate they seemed to me to be sitting there sniffing.

On the green light we crossed Saint Catherine and pulled up in front of the Metro station at De Maisonneuve. The door hissed open and feet clomped up onto the bus, tickets were dropped into the slot, transfers changed hands, small change clattered into the box. The mouth of the Metro station disgorged more humans who climbed onto the bus. The bus was filling up, but a glance to my left showed me there were still a few seats at the back. The door shut and we moved off, getting jammed into the traffic before reaching Sherbrooke and being forced to inch along.

There was a man standing in front of me, I could see him over the top of my painting. He was in his late fifties, a sharp-faced man with a military mustache.

"Would you move over, don't take two places," he said.

I was not taking two places, I was taking a place and a half, and this was obviously because of all the things I had with me. I pulled my bag of groceries closer, I pressed harder against the end of the seat. The man sat down, squeezing himself in.

"Why don't you put that bag on your knee," he said. "People want to sit down."

"I've got things on my knee," I said. "And I have to hold my painting."

"Some people think they own the seats on these buses," he said.

"You've got a seat," I said. "What more do you want?"

Suddenly the two old women were talking, and quite loudly.

"What do you expect from that kind?" said one, following this with a remark that, if it were not true, I would never think of making up—"*Dirty hippie!*"

She was referring to me!

"It's about time someone stood up to them," said the other.

"Characters like this think they own the world," the man said out of the side of his mouth, the side the women were on.

The bus had become absolutely silent except for the speakers.

"Look at that hair. Did you ever see anything like it?" said one of the women.

"It's disgraceful! Something should be done about them."

"If one of my grandchildren ever got like that I'd skin him alive. They shouldn't be allowed on the streets."

"They'd all be in jail if I had anything to say about it."

I was a witness to what followed. You will understand I was driven to it. You can imagine me sitting there having to hear myself vilified in such a fashion, and so unjustly, and with a full bus straining their ears to catch every word—not that they had to strain hard because my seat companions *meant* to be heard by everyone. The bus had crossed Sherbrooke and was moving up Cote des Neiges Road (which is still Guy Street but the name changes at this point, if you didn't know that), and they kept babbling away and pouring out venom on me relentlessly. Everyone was staring at me. The man was squeezed in beside me, making little comments sideways at the women, agreeing with all they said and adding his own brilliant observations, no doubt feeling very heroic for having stood up to the hippie menace. All of a sudden—for by now I'd had enough; I'd been trying to put a good face on the day, but you can only deprive a man of so much—I shot my hand across his face and up, passing an inch from his nose, and reaching as if to pull the stop cord. He jumped about a foot off his seat. "I thought this was my stop," I said, withdrawing my hand. In fact it *was* my stop, we were coming to MacGregor, but I didn't ring the bell. Instead I started sniffing loudly. Then I boomed out in the biggest voice I could manage:

"Listen, mister, I don't like to bring this up in public, but did you ever smell yourself? You smell like you shit your pants. God! It's been torture sitting here. I mean you *stink*. Couldn't you wait till you got home?"

His jaw fell, he was so startled; then he turned a couple of shades of purple. He started to reply but the incongruity had confused him, since it was supposed to be *him* talking about *me* being filthy, not the other way around.

"You—you—don't you—don't you talk about —you filthy hippie—you—"Stammering and spluttering like that. Naturally the women took into exclaiming "Well I never" and "Of all the nerve!"

"And you!" I boomed, while I was at it. "My golly, you'd think ladies your age would learn something about *cleanliness*. Look at you, the dirt on your faces, your lines and wrinkles are all caked with crud. And you're no bouquet of roses either. You smell like this panhandler beside me. Weren't any of you ever toilet trained?"

Well, they commenced screaming and howling and setting up a terrible protest, faces contorted and murderous. All three were going together, beside themselves with outrage and indignation; they had never been so mortified. While their counter-insults got jumbled up with each other I was carrying on in a great heavy voice saying things like:

"I certainly wouldn't let *my* parents out on the street in your condition. It should be a crime to subject innocent people like myself to such disgusting body odours. Have you no sense of decency? Are you so oblivious to the senses of others? Do you actually *like* to be dirty and smell that bad? It's enough to make a person throw up."

"I've never heard we do not smell I'll have you know took a bath before I left home this morning don't bother with him the impudent you're the one who stinks look at you long filthy hair young bum I wash every day she doesn't smell never been so insulted something should be done about how dare I never heard—"

I clamped my fingers onto my nose and stuck my tongue out. "I'm going to puke!" I said. "I'm going to puke all over you." The little man beside me went into a panic; he was squeezed in tight and tried to bolt up but couldn't move. "No, wait—it's okay," I said. "I can hold it. I'll hold my nose, I can't breathe this stench any longer. I think I'd better get off next stop before I suffocate."

"I ought to—ought to—I ought to—" the man was saying, quivering and shaking and going on as if completely unhinged.

One astonishing thing about all this was the bus driver. He was sitting only a few feet away and never once turned his head but continued driving on. I heard one of the women demanding that I be ejected from the bus but he paid no attention. As for the other passengers, before getting off I gave a quick look back at them. There were indifferent expressions and a good many hostile ones. I decided I would accept the indifferents as being on my side, though it's highly likely I was alone in my fight, for who can have sympathy for a youth who insults his elders?

Bertha And Bill

Bertha Northrup is one of the more unusual poets around Montreal. She was born without arms and does her writing and typing with her toes. A few years ago Weekend Magazine did an article on her with pictures of her using her feet for all sorts of things you'd normally use hands for.

Bertha's mother (who's now dead) took great pains to teach her to be self-sufficient so today Bertha is able to get along pretty much like any of us, or at least about as efficiently.

In May of last year a young poet by the name of Bill Lewis came up from Glace Bay, Nova Scotia. Bill stands an easy six-eight and weighs maybe a hundred and twenty pounds and he has bulbous eyes and a receding chin and a face covered with acne. Before coming to Montreal he didn't drink much but since the rest of us like to take a drop he started doing the same.

On a Friday night we were in a tavern. We thought we'd introduce Bill to Bertha. We left in a lively mood, arguing and singing and belching, and when we got to Bertha's place on Aylmer street she let us in, opening the door with her toes. As soon as we were settled she brought out the beer. For someone unfamiliar with Bertha it was a sight to watch her get the drinks. She took the glasses from a low cupboard and the beers from the fridge, and then popped them open with an opener and poured them into the glasses... all the time using her toes. Her legs were very supple and she could use her toes practically like fingers. She was fully competent and once you'd been around a while you hardly noticed that she had no arms. She sat on the couch drinking, holding the glass with one foot, and in the other foot she held a cigarette. She often wore dresses so, if you were interested in that sort of thing, you could see her panties with most of the moves she made. She wasn't really bad looking, somewhat along the lines of Venus de Milo.

Bill was quite taken with her. He stared at every move she made, his bulging eyes bulging even more than usual, hardly able to believe what he saw.

"Why, you're amazing," he said. "I've never seen anything like this before in my whole life. Where'd you learn to do all those things? Boy, that's really something." He sat there shaking his head in awe. "And you write poems. Let me read some of your poetry."

She gave Bill some of her verses to read. Most of Bertha's poems were feminine little things, wistfully romantic. "Here you are with no arms, and you write better poetry than I do," Bill said. "This is great stuff."

Then he read a short story she'd written, about a flower that could walk, and he covered this with as much praise as her verse.

"I knew I'd run into talent when I came to Montreal," he said, "but I never pictured anything like this. Boy, I've got a lot of catching up to do." While he was reading Bertha's writings he was pouring down her beer. He got settled on the couch beside her and they were soon engaged in a deep discussion. In the meantime, we were also drinking Bertha's beer, and a bottle of rum we'd brought along with us, courtesy of Richard Archangel, as he called himself. His real name was Richard Hogg, which he wasn't very fond of. Besides Richard there was Moe Caron, who didn't write poems but played drums in a rock band; Jack Pittman, a Newfoundlander who was leaving in a few days for South America, the last I saw of him; and myself, Sam McCarthy. It was a normal gathering for us guys, we sat around and got fairly loaded, and argued about one thing and another. We didn't get too much contribution from Bill or Bertha because they were too busy with their own conversation.

Later on when most of the liquor was gone we decided it was time to go.

"I'll stick around a bit," Bill said. "Bertha and I got too much to talk about. I can find my way home. This is the most interesting girl I ever met."

Bertha smiled, looking pleased, so we left the two of them together and departed.

"They make a lovely pair," Richard remarked when we were out on the street.

Evidently they did, at least for that night. A couple of evenings later Bill came to my place, and he was solemn. I was curious about what had happened at Bertha's after the rest of us left, but I didn't want to bring the subject up out of delicacy.

But since Bill didn't look like he was going to bring it up himself, I said, "Well, did you have a good talk with Bertha the other night?"

He looked at me morosely. "Don't mention it," he said.

"Why, what happened?"

"Nothing."

"What time did you leave? It was pretty late when the rest of us pulled out."

"I don't know," he said. "I guess I stayed there all night."

I was going to say "Oho!" but I didn't, because this was a case of a girl with no arms, which is not quite the ordinary situation. For instance, she was defenceless, if Bill had tried something.

"Have you seen her since?" I said.

"No."

"What do you think of her? She's quite a girl, isn't she?"

"Yeah, I guess so."

"You guess so? A couple of nights ago you were raving about how talented she is."

"Well," he said, "I was drunk."

"You don't think too much of her now, I take it."

214

"Listen, I was drunk," he said, obviously reluctant to continue with the conversation.

"Okay, so we'll forget it," I said. "So you were drunk, you got carried away, and no doubt you threw one into her, and now you're sorry."

He jumped up, almost hitting the ceiling. "I never said that."

"All right, you didn't."

He sat down again. "I shouldn't get drunk like that," he said, looking very mournful.

"Ah, then you did?"

"Well, so maybe I did. But I was drunk as hell. In the morning I didn't know what had happened or where I was. I thought I was in a nightmare. I got nothing against girls with no arms, but it gave me an awful shock. I don't even like to think about it. She called me up today and wants me to come over and see her. I told her I couldn't make it. I don't want to get mixed up in this."

I could see he was very much bothered about it, not only about sleeping with Bertha, but because he wasn't big enough to be able to take it in stride. It was obvious he felt he was being prejudiced. I said:

"So what's wrong with Bertha? She mightn't have any arms but she's a nice girl, and she's not bad to look at either. Why don't you go see her tonight?"

He sat there with a long face, his shoulders slumped.

"I know. That's what I should do. You're right," he said. "But I don't want this to go any further. I don't want to get messed up in some kind of relationship with her. You don't know what it's like because it's not you that's involved. You can sit there and be big about it but you haven't slept with her."

"How do you know?" I said.

"Well, did you?"

I admitted I hadn't, but told him it didn't matter. I said he'd done Bertha a fine service, because it wasn't that easy for her to get a man. On top of that, I said, he'd probably done himself a service, because despite the fact she had no arms Bertha was probably good tail, as the sexologists say.

"It's only prejudice that stops other guys from getting some good enjoyment from a real nice girl," I said. "I'd go after her myself if I didn't already have a woman."

"Yeah, sure."

"Well, why not? Nobody's ever said Venus de Milo's not an attractive woman. She doesn't have any arms. Moreover I don't think Bertha's interested in me. You're the first guy I've seen that she really took to."

He looked at me suspiciously. "What are you trying to do, anyway?"

"I'm not trying to do anything. I just think you're a pretty phony poet if you've got prejudices against a handicapped person."

"It's not prejudice. I'm not prejudiced against anybody. I'm not prejudiced against elephants but I don't have to sleep with one, do I? You're taking this all wrong, that's all. You can sit there and look liberal and charitable because it doesn't concern you. But you didn't sleep with Bertha."

216

"Wasn't it good?" I said.

"Well, it wasn't bad, except she had her feet up around my face and was running her toes through my hair, and that was a bit strange. Jesus." He shook his head. "I don't remember anything very well because I was so drunk. I was going like an old stallion and she was wriggling and twisting around like a worm. I hardly knew where she was half the time. You know what I'm like, long and gangly, and she's pretty small anyway aside from having no arms. After we finished she started crying for some reason, but she stopped after a while and seemed in good enough spirits. Then we went to sleep. I suppose I said all kinds of idiotic things to her though I can't remember what they were. When I woke up I had my arms around her. My head was pounding and my mouth was dry and I felt just miserable. I looked at the girl I was holding onto and I couldn't believe my eyes. For about three minutes I couldn't remember the night before and I thought I was going crazy. I was brought up in a pretty ordinary family where everybody had all their arms and legs and you didn't think about having sex with anyone, let alone a freak. Now, I'm not calling Bertha a freak, because I don't think that way now, but when I was brought up a girl with no arms was a freak, and soon as I woke up and looked at her, that was my natural thought. I tried to collect my wits, though I could hardly think of anything because my head was in such bad condition. And then Bertha woke up. Well, I remembered then about the previous evening, and I did my best to carry things through. I complained about how bad I felt and she jumped up and said she'd get me a coffee. So I got out of bed and washed and got dressed and went into the kitchen where she was making coffee with her toes. You know, pouring the water and putting in milk and sugar and stirring it. Boy, just think now, how strange this was." Bill was staring at the wall all the time he was talking. He looked over at me, then looked back at the wall. "Okay, so I gulped down some coffee and then I said I had to leave right away. I had to go see somebody, I said. She saw me to the door and I got out of there, and when I hit the pavement I was some glad. I wanted to get away from that place and forget about everything. I felt lousy all day, afraid she'd feel she had some hold on me, and that she'd be expecting me to take this thing further. I felt I'd got into something. It wasn't good, that business, but it might be all right if it blew over and nothing more came of it. But then she called me today and asked if I'd like to come and see her. What am I going to do? I don't want to hurt her, and I don't like myself for not going to see her, but just the same..."

He was clearly in a worried state. I offered him a beer but he said he didn't want to drink anymore, not for the time being at least. He said he was thinking of going back to Nova Scotia. I told him matters weren't that serious, that he could be friends with Bertha without getting involved in a serious relationship.

"What if she's pregnant?" he said. "I didn't have any safes with me and I was too drunk to care. I doubt if she's on the pill. I mean, I'm pretty sure she's not."

"Well, that could turn out to be a problem, but hope for the best," I advised.

He went away, as disconsolate as ever. As he left I recommended that his experience might prove valuable as material for a few good poems later on, but he just looked at me. He wasn't in a poetic frame of mind.

Later on, as I was having a beer and waiting for Diane, my girlfriend, to show up—we were going to some movie or other—the phone rang. It was Bertha.

"Have you seen your friend Bill lately?" she said. I had the usual mental picture of her holding the phone in her toes, it was hard to get away from.

"I was talking to him for a while earlier," I said.

"Did he say anything about me?"

"Well, he did mention that he'd stayed at your place the other night," I said.

"Is that all he said?"

"More or less. That about sums it up."

"He was awfully drunk."

"Yeah, he doesn't hold his liquor too good."

"He wanted to stay the night, so I let him. I don't think he could have gotten home by himself. He certainly does rave on, once he gets talking. Do you think he has the makings of a poet?"

"I don't know. Some of his things look promising, but I can't say. We'll have to wait and see."

"I hope he does have some success. He's something like Alexander Pope in reverse, don't you think? He's so long and skinny and he's really not very handsome. His face is in quite bad condition. It's terrible the way acne affects some people. I feel sorry for him, don't you?"

"I haven't thought too much about it, but I suppose he's got some things working against him."

"He lives by himself in a little room, he said."

"Yeah, he's got a place on Jeanne Mance. It's pretty small, but it's cheap. He can hardly lie down in it without bending his knees."

"That's too bad. It must be hard for him, coming to Montreal after living in a small town with his parents. I feel a little sorry for the guy."

"He'll manage. He's not too helpless."

"But we should do what we can to make him feel at home here. I know if I were a stranger in Montreal I wouldn't know where to turn."

"Well, he'll get used to it."

"I called him today and asked him over, but he said he was busy. I don't think he really was, but he's a very shy boy. He practically stuttered over the phone. And you should have seen him when he left here the other morning. He hardly said a word, and kept looking at the floor. He hardly knew what to do with himself. I don't think he makes friends easily, and it would be nice if we could help him"

"He's not in that bad shape, Bertha."

"Well, how would you feel if you looked like him and had to walk down the street? I'm sure people stare at him. He's probably very sensitive. He must be or he wouldn't be a poet. I probably sound like a mother hen or something but I'd like to help him along if I can. You should too. The next time you see him tell him that any time he wants to come over and talk about poetry or anything, that I'll be glad to see him. And be sure to invite him to your place as often as you can. Okay?"

"All right, Bertha. I'll do that."

But I didn't see Bill for a while after that. He kind of dropped out of sight for a while.

Man With A Flair

Perhaps you wonder what I'm thinking about, sitting here in the Black Horse tavern every day, a grey-headed man with a faraway look in his eye. Maybe you've heard of me—Hazen Bass. I worked at the pulp mill years ago, before getting fired for drinking on the job, supposedly.

Maybe it was true, but who wouldn't drink when their hopes have died and turned to dust on the Boulevard of Broken Dreams?

I'm not a stupid man, no matter what you think.

A couple of years after I left the pulp mill the wife Winnie ran off with my one-time friend, Bill Muster. She took everything with her—kids, furniture, knives, forks, cups, plates—everything but the wall-paper. She even took the garbage can and left the garbage.

I remember her chucking my favorite chair onto the back of Bill's truck. Bill had the nerve to come along and help her clean me out. Seeing my chair go with all the rest he looked embarrassed and shook his head, as if to say, "That's a woman for you! Always up to something." Like he was in the moving business and had nothing to do with it.

She rammed the tailgate to, rolled down her sleeves and turned on me for the final time. "I only got two good things to say about you, you drunken bum. Goodbye and good riddance! I was a fool to marry you in the first place. If you hadn't taken advantage of me, a poor girl that didn't know no better..."

That's how life slaps you in the face. What they mean by salt in the wounds.

When I think of what I sacrificed for that woman, only to have her turn around and treat me like a dog. Telling me I took advantage of her! I remember that night, don't worry. Her feeding me wine until I couldn't see straight and then grappling me to the floor and ripping my trousers off. "Hazen, please! You know we shouldn't do this..." Well, I married her, didn't I? One mistake and my whole life ruined. Instead of Hollywood... Bannonbridge. Instead of the Silver Screen, the pulp mill. To this day I can hear her voice whining in my ears. "You and your big talk! Always going on about what you coulda been. You make me sick! Go on, get outa me sight! You ain't dragging me down to the gutter with you..."

She was wrong, of course. I get by with my little business. I've got a nice line of samples—they're right here, I'll show you in a minute. Nobody can say I don't know how to take care of myself.

Yet it all could have been so different.

I was a great reader as a young man, back in the days before TV. I read books by the dozen. Luke Short was my favorite—I read every western he ever wrote.

And movies... As a kid I'd go to the Capitol theatre on Saturday afternoons, and all week I'd be Randolph Scott or John Wayne or Tarzan or Jungle Jim. I saw every show that came around on Saturday. Westerns, horrors, comedies, crime, you name it.

I knew about books and movies, and I could imagine things. But above all, which was the crowning touch, I had a flair. My Grade Nine teacher, Mrs. Maloney, told me I had a flair. She used to assign us essays to write, and when she read what I wrote about "Heroes of the Old West," she said, "Hazen, you have *a flair for writing*." Her exact words.

I don't know about you, but it tells me something. What it tells me is if it hadn't been for Winnie I could have married Marilyn Monroe or Elizabeth Taylor. That if fate hadn't cruelly interfered there'd probably be a statue of me in the park today beside Lord Beaverbrook's—it was that close.

Now do you understand? When you see that faraway look in my eye, it's just my mind drifting back to better days, to what might have been. To the day I walked into the Black Horse and found Howard Perley there. And he began telling me about the time he'd been a screenwriter in Hollywood.

§

Howard's dead now, he turned yellow and passed away, but back then he had some spunk left in him. He was about fifty and a salesman with his own line of goods and, as far as I could tell, his office was the Black Horse. You could always find him there with his battered case on the floor beside him. He sold things like combs and tooth brushes and French safes and ladies silk stockings.

Although I'd seen him around often enough, I'd never talked to him. People said he was an educated man with a degree from St. Thomas University and that he'd travelled all over the world. He was a man of mystery. A tarnished diamond in the rough.

Earlier that afternoon, on my way to the tavern, I'd stopped at the town library and picked up an armload of westerns.

Howard was sitting at the next table by himself and he leaned over and examined one of my books.

"You like to read, do you, son?"

"Quite a bit," I replied. "I got laid off last week so there's not much else to do." I was an aimless youth in those days, working at various jobs here and there, still undecided on a career in life.

Howard bent closer and said, "Then you must be a romantic."

"What?" I slid my chair back a little. "I don't know about that," I said. "The girlfriend doesn't think so. Winnie says that's the trouble with me, I never bring her flowers or stuff."

"That's not what I meant, exactly. Any man who reads novels is a romantic. A dreamer. I'll bet you have dreams. Am I right?"

"What kind of dreams?"

"Dreams of glory—of fame and fortune. I had them myself at your age. I was a reader then, too... I loved books. As a matter of fact I wrote a couple myself, at one time, before I went to Hollywood. Ever been to Hollywood? A young man like yourself, you ought to go to Hollywood. Only don't make the mistakes I made." He tipped up his glass even though it was empty. "Damn. You know, I went and left my wallet home? I'm getting forgetful in my old age."

"That's okay. I'll get you one," I said.

"That's very kind of you." He looked at his watch and slid over to a chair at my table. "I should be out making some calls, but what the hell. There's always time for another."

It turned out he had time for quite a few others. Though to tell the truth I was so taken by the things he told me I hardly noticed myself paying for them.

"Yes, I had it all once," he was saying. "Success, money, women. A house in Beverly Hills. A swimming pool, a tennis court, two maids, a butler. A Rolls Royce and a uniformed chauffeur. A couple of sports cars. I was pulling in five hundred grand a year, and that was real money in those days, not like today. And of course the girls. There was never a shortage of those in Hollywood. You've probably seen some of them on the big screen."

226

The Black Horse Tavern

I'd read about people like Howard, men with a past, who'd come down in the world. His clothes alone told a story. He was wearing a suit and tie, but they were old and threadbare, like something off the rack at the Sally Ann. He hadn't shaved for a couple of days, and the first thing he did—once he had his beer—was borrow some tobacco off me to roll himself a smoke. He said he'd forgotten his cigarettes.

"You were in Hollywood?" I said, my interest aroused. Most of the men you met in the tavern, the only place they'd ever been was somewhere like Bathurst, or maybe Moncton. And all they talked about was cars and trucks and baseball and hockey. "What'd you do there? What happened? How come you didn't stay?"

"Well, it's an old story, I wasn't the first screenwriter to get kicked out of town. It all started when I published my second book, a crime novel called... if I can remember, now... *Death Of A Salesman*. You ever read it?"

"I don't think so. But it sounds familiar."

"One of Marilyn's husbands, Art Miller, stole the title off me for a play he did. Anyhow, the phone rang and I got invited out to Hollywood and signed to a contract. I worked on quite a few movies and the money poured in... I was a hot property there for a while. But to make a long story short, the fast life got the best of me, too much booze and gambling and too many girls. Hanging out with characters like Scott Fitzgerald—or Fitz, as I called him. Next thing I got behind on my scripts and the studio boss, Jack Warner,

227

called me into his office. He warned me but I just laughed him off. I was too cocky for my own good. I said, 'Sure, Jack, whatever you say...' The next morning I rolled in drunk and when he tried to send me home I blew my stack.

"Now that was a scene straight from Hollywood! I threw a chair through the window and picked Jack up by the seat of the pants and threw him out after it.

"I was finished from that day on. The studios blacklisted me and I couldn't get work anywhere. It was pretty bad, because by this time I'd run up some heavy debts. Finally I slipped out of town and went on the bum for a while. I rode the boxcars from California to New York City, living in hobo jungles. In New York I started a few businesses, made and lost a few fortunes, until I got tired of the rat race and decided to come home. Since then, as you probably know, I've been in sales."

He paused. I thought he was remembering his lost youth, but he said, "Speaking of sales, are you okay for safes? I've got a shipment coming in Thursday. I can give you a good deal on a gross..."

If only I'd met him a few months earlier!

His was a fascinating story, a tragedy. I couldn't help but pity the man. But in the back of my mind an idea had begun to take hold.

"It must've been great out there in Hollywood," I said. "I mean, before you got fired and everything."

"It was great alright. That's the trouble. Once you've had a job like that it's hard to settle into anything else. It's why I've had so many up and downs. I can't get over my years in Hollywood."

"I guess a guy'd have to be pretty handy, to do a job like writing movies?"

"Well, it takes a certain type. Someone like yourself, now, who reads books and likes the pictures... You might have a chance. You like the pictures, don't you?"

"I go every chance I get."

"You mind?" He took my pack of tobacco and rolled himself another cigarette.

"Now, I had no training," he was saying. "Never took a writing course in my life. But I could sit down and run off a scenario in half an hour and sell it for, oh, thirty thousand bucks easy. You know what a scenario is, don't you?"

It sounded Spanish to me. Like senorita.

Seeing the blank look on my face he said, "It's like the general idea what the movie's going to be about. You throw in a few facts, a description or two, a bit of talk. Enough to give the drift of the story. There's nothing to it once you know how."

He picked up his empty glass and looked it over and put it down again.

"Sorry," I said. I drained mine and ordered a couple more. Eventually I got up the courage to ask him if he could help me, say, if I wanted to become a screenwriter myself, maybe.

"Well, I *could*," he said. "But it's the kind of thing you mostly have to learn on your own, by practice. I could give you some hints, but if you don't work at it all the help in the world won't matter."

I told him that back in Grade Nine my English teacher had complimented me on my essay writing, telling me I had a flair.

"A flair?" said Howard.

"That's right. A flair for writing."

He suggested the best way for me to start was to check the Capitol for a movie coming up next week, one I hadn't seen.

"Take down the name of some movie and go home and write your own script, right out of your head. Then go see the picture and you can judge how you did. You can learn a lot that way and it'll give you experience. Experience is the important thing. You need that experience."

"Okay," I said. "And then what?"

"Well, if you did a bad job, quit. Or try again. If you did a good job, write yourself up an original movie and send it to a studio in Hollywood, and maybe you'll get hired."

I wanted to rush out and get at it right away, but he held me back.

"There's no hurry," he said. "You been drinking all afternoon, and one thing you have to learn is you can't write when you're drinking. It ruins the concentration. Do it tomorrow. Right now let's have another beer and we can discuss things some more."

It was ten at night before I got out of there, by which time all my money was gone. Howard stayed behind talking baseball with a couple of young guys my age. It turned out he'd been a baseball scout, too, for the New York Yankees. He was just getting into that as I left. Personally I've never cared that much about baseball.

As I weaved my way homeward my head was filled with visions of the future. Howard had been a Godsend. Until meeting him I'd been unsure what to do with my life. Now I knew, and it was a thrilling feeling. A young man finally finding his calling in life...

In my excited imagination I was a brilliant screenwriter already. I had my sports cars, my yacht, my butler and my maid, everything money could buy.

I had no delusions about Howard. He was over the hill these days, no more than a shadow of his former self. But he'd been there once and knew what he was talking about.

He'd been places and done things others only dream about. How many men can say they've spent a night with Marilyn Monroe?

When he told me that I was dumbfounded.

"Look, kid," he said, "it's no big deal. Remember, we're talking about Hollywood. All these movie stars are the same. If you can do something for them they don't think twice about coming across. Marilyn was after me to write a script for her, something up her alley, so I said come on over and we'll talk about it. When we climbed out of bed next morning I told her I had a few ideas. I was pretty busy but I'd see what I could do. Then she went and met Art Miller. Art wrote her a script and next thing you know they're married, for a few months. But it could've been me in his place. If I hadn't been so damned busy—or so damned drunk, one or the other."

Anyone could see it was his weakness for the bottle that brought him down. I promised myself I'd never make the same mistake, not if I got to Hollywood.

Next morning with my head in the toilet bowl I wasn't so sure of myself as the night before. But a few beers brought me round, and I found I was still resolved to give it a try. "What've I got to lose?" I thought. "Others have done it, so why not me?"

My father worked at the pulp mill back then, he'd been there day in and day out, year after year, and in my opinion it was a life of pure drudgery. If you were going to escape that kind of future you had to think big and take chances. Try the things that most people wouldn't even talk about.

In my mind I saw guys like me trudging off to the mill, while down in Hollywood some bigshot was throwing his hands up in the air. "I wish to hell I could get me a half-decent script!" he's saying. At that moment his secretary brings in the mail, and there's an envelope from one Hazen Bass, otherwise known as yours truly, who instead of choosing a life of drudgery pulled up his sox and produced the goods.

§

It happened to be a few days before Halloween, and the posters on the Capitol were advertising a triple bill of horror movies: *Billy the Kid vs. Dracula,*

Godzilla Takes On The Thing, and *Jesse James Meets Frankenstein's Daughter*. Luckily I'd never seen any of them before.

Two in particular caught my fancy, because of the cowboys in them. Even though I'd seen my share of horror shows, westerns were my favourites, and I figured I could handle one of these the best.

It only took me a minute to make up my mind. It wasn't that I didn't like Billy the Kid, but the Jesse movie had a woman in it, and in the movies they always like to have some kind of romance thrown in.

The outlaw hero and the daughter of Frankenstein. When I think of it now, it was sort of like myself and Winnie.

That afternoon I arrived at the Black Horse and found Howard in his usual place with an empty glass in front of him. The veins on his face lit up when he saw me.

"So, how's the script coming?" he said.

"I got it here," I said, taking out my sheets of paper.

"Already?"

"You said you could do one in half an hour. I must've put in at least twice that long."

He shook his head. "No, no, my boy. I was talking about a scenario, not a script. You can't do a proper script in half an hour. The fastest I did one was three days and it almost killed me. I'll tell you about it sometime." He patted his pockets. "I was thinking... Look, you don't have the price of a beer on you, do you?"

233

"Sure." I'd been cleaned out the night before, but I'd stopped at the bank on my way over. I used to be able to do that, put a little away in the bank for a rainy day.

I ordered a couple, and said, "You said you were thinking."

"Thinking? I can't remember. Anyway, let's have a look at what you wrote."

"Well," I said, suddenly feeling a little shy, "to be honest, it's not actually *finished*. I just thought I'd show you the start I made so you could tell me how I'm doing."

He pulled out an old pair of glasses with one of the shafts broken off.

"You remind me of myself," he said, "what I was like in the old days. Couldn't wait to get to the top."

Picking up the pages he began to read.

JESSE JAMES MEETS FRANKENSTEIN'S DAUGHTER:
A Movie By Hazen Bass

Jesse and his brother Frank and the gang are sitting on their horses behind a foothill. A few yards away is the railroad track with a big tree sitting across it. The horses snort and paw the ground. Everyone's anxious for the train to come.

They hear a train hoot. It comes nearer. It rounds the bend and the engineer sees the tree and slams on the brakes. The train stops inches from the fallen tree.

At that moment the gang rides out firing their guns in the air.

"Train robbery! It's Jesse James!"

The message moves quick as lightning through the train and the passengers tremble and try to hide their valuables.

In a minute the gang is aboard the train. The trainmen who try to resist are shot down.

"Don't try nothin' foolish and nobody'll git hurt," says Jesse. "Jist relax and empty yer pockets." The gang moves down the aisles collecting wallets, watches and jewelery.

One of the gang, a roughneck bandit named Jack Slade, snickers at a pretty girl as he takes her necklace.

"Yer a mighty purdy girl," he says. "Too bad I gotta take this on ya. Har! har!"

"You monster!" squeals the girl.

From the back of the car comes a rough female voice: "Is someone calling me?"

"Jess, lookit that!" whispers Frank, his hair standing on end. The woman who spoke has got to her feet and is lumbering down the aisle. She's over eight feet tall and weighs a good four hundred pounds. There's a spike sticking out of her head, and her face is covered with stitches like she's just had an operation.

Yes... Frankenstein's daughter!

Jack Slade gives her a cool look. "All right, sister, sit yerself down. Nobody's a-callin' you."

Snorting like a bear the young woman keeps walking towards him.

"I don't like to shoot no girl," says Slade, "but if you mosey another step closer I'll drill ya full of lead."

The monster girl stops about ten feet away. Around her neck is a string of diamond-studded hearts. The camera moves up so you can see them better. They're human hearts! She clutches the necklace protectively.

"Are you gonna take my jewellery?"

"I don't play no favourites," says Slade. "Hand it over here."

"I won't! You can't have it!"

"Yeah, and why not?"

"Cuz you can't."

"Oh yeah?"

"Yeah."

"Sez who?"

"Me!"

She starts to come closer.

"I warned ya, lady." Slade pumps two shots into her but the girl doesn't bat an eye.

"Tarnation!" gasps Frank. He shudders and drops his gun and jumps out the train window.

Jesse catches hold of Slade. "You lowdown yellow-bellied varmint. That ain't no way to treat a lady." Slade pulls away from him and drills two more shots into the girl. Nothing happens. It's like shooting at a bale of hay.

"Okay," says Slade. "Keep yer dad-blamed necklace. I didn't want it nohow."

"No, and ya ain't gonna want this neither, but yer a-gittin' it!" says Jesse, and lands an uppercut that sends Slade cart-wheeling.

236

The girl stops. A horrible grin splits her face. She pats her hair into place, gives Jesse a coy look.

"Ya gotta excuse him, ma'am," says Jesse. "He ain't one of the reg'lar gang. He jined us back in Witchita and I never knowed nothin' bout him. Man's got no sensa decency."

"You're my kinda man," she says. "Whyncha come up and see me sometime?"

"Might jist do that, one of these days. If I'm packing a ladder. How's the weather up there? Har! Har! Now back to yer seat, miss. We gotta lighten you folks of yer valables and hit the trail."

Later, as the gang is riding off with saddlebags stuffed with loot, Frank appears from behind a foothill and gallops up to Jesse.

"Jesse," he gasps, his face white as a sheet. "That... (gulp) that-that-that... that-that..."

"Yeah," says Jesse, "a nice chunka woman-flesh. Quite a looker, but I ain't got time fer no wimmin jist yet. I reckon she's the new schoolmarm I heard was a-comin' to these here parts. Sophistycated, like, fancy jewlry and all, and them purdy ways."

"I mean the one—Dagnabit, Slade done shot her twice in the heart—the one—"

"Yeah, I hear ya. With the spike in her head. What'll they think of next, eh, Frank? The way wimmin gits theirselves up these days! Still, a man's a fool to judge a book by its cover... Gal like that, ya show her a chuckwagon and she might jist rustle up a mess of vittles to have yer tongue a-hangin' out. S'pose we'll ever run into her agin?"

Little did he know.

Their voices fade as they gallop off into the sunset, heading down the trail towards Carson City...

Howard set the pages down. He drained his glass and chewed on his lip for a moment, as if unconscious of my future hanging in the balance. I fidgeted in my chair. It was all I could do to breathe.

"Son," he said at last, "you'd better hold onto your hat. This is the finest cowboy-horror script I've read in many a year."

I let out a sigh of relief.

"You really mean it?" I said.

"Of course I mean it! Only a man with a flair could have produced such a work. Let me shake your hand." He reached his hand across the table and I shook it. "You got a bright future ahead of you, young fellow. If you play your cards right you could go a long way in the industry. By George, if my glass wasn't empty I'd drink to it!"

Flushed with excitement I called out to the waiter. "Bring us four!"

§

The following night Winnie gave me her news, and being an honourable man I accepted my responsibility and did the right thing. Her father threatening to shoot me had nothing to do with it. The rest of the story you know. I found a steady job at the pulp mill, and every day after work you'd see me heading for the

Black Horse, too tired and disgusted with my life to do anything else. And so the years went by.

Today I'm as old as Howard was when I met him. And today, like Howard, when my wallet happens to be light—when sales in combs and tooth brushes, French safes and ladies silk stockings are slow—and I spot a young man with a certain something walk in the tavern door, I sit him down and encourage his dream. I tell him of the great days in Hollywood, the many fine scripts I wrote, and the fortune that slipped through my fingers, and how I almost married Raquel Welch. I see it all, as we sit there and drink, that glorious past, see it as vividly as Howard did in his time. And perhaps, for all anyone knows, as this youth will in his.

Raymond Fraser is the author of twelve books of fiction, three of non-fiction, and six collections of poetry. His novel *The Bannonbridge Musicians* was runner-up for the Governor General's Award. In 2009 following publication of his novel *In Another Life* he received the Lieutenant-Governor's Award for High Achievement in English Language Literary Arts. Five of his books are listed in *Atlantic Canada's 100 Greatest Books*. In 2012 he was appointed to the Order of New Brunswick for his contributions to literature and culture in the province.
http://raymondfraser.blogspot.com